K
in

Th[...]
he[...]
resis[...]

"Quinn." His [...] her lips. "I wish things were d[...]

"I do, too."

Kissing her would be a simple matter of capturing her mouth with his. He didn't, though his gut told him she'd respond with an ardor she kept hidden.

"I… um…" She hesitated.

"Right." Hadn't he vowed mere minutes ago to avoid causing her trouble?

Quinn retreated a step, then walked away. Mistakes were easy to make, and he'd committed too many already in his life.

4 1 0260989 0

RESCUING THE COWBOY

BY
CATHY McDAVID

First Published in Great Britain 2016
By Mills & Boon, an imprint of HarperCollins*Publishers*
1 London Bridge Street, London, SE1 9GF

© 2016 Cathy McDavid

ISBN: 978-0-263-92030-7

23-1016

Our policy is to use papers that are natural, renewable and recyclable products and made from wood grown in sustainable forests. The logging and manufacturing processes conform to the legal environmental regulations of the country of origin.

Printed and bound in Spain
by CPI, Barcelona

Since 2006, *New York Times* bestselling author **Cathy McDavid** has been happily penning contemporary Westerns for Mills & Boon. Every day, she gets to write about handsome cowboys riding the range or busting a bronc. It's a tough job, but she's willing to make the sacrifice. Cathy shares her Arizona home with her own real-life sweetheart and a trio of odd pets. Her grown twins have left to embark on lives of their own, and she couldn't be prouder of their accomplishments.

To Mike, as always.
What they say is true,
it only takes a moment.

Chapter One

Shopping in a small-town market shouldn't be a nightmare. Four thousand square feet. Three aisles crammed with merchandise. A modest dairy and meat department. Fresh produce on Wednesdays: be sure and get there early before it's all gone. A completely uneventful and uninteresting excursion for most people.

But not for Summer Goodwyn. Yet, what choice did she have? She'd promised to bring homemade oatmeal cookies—without raisins—to the party later today at Dos Estrellas Ranch. After a thorough search of her pantry had netted only half the necessary ingredients, a trip to the market couldn't be avoided.

Oatmeal without raisins was the only kind of cookies her son, Teddy, ate. If she offered him something else, he might have a meltdown, and that would ruin the party.

She glanced down at him, sitting in the shopping cart basket, shoulders hunched. His rhythmic back and forth motion could be a good thing. He often rocked for hours to soothe himself. Or it could be a warning sign of things to come.

"I was thinking you might want to wear your new blue shirt today." Blue was his favorite color.

Teddy didn't answer. Rather, he stared at nothing in particular, his eyes barely visible beneath an unruly fringe of reddish-blond hair. Teddy hated going to the barber shop, although the elderly gentleman who cut his hair was very understanding.

Maybe she should call and beg off the party. On second thought, that wasn't an option. The Dempseys were good to Summer. Really good. Without them, there'd be no equine therapy program for Teddy and other children like him. Plus, the party was special: a welcome to Mustang Valley for Josh and Cole's cousin who'd arrived a few days ago. The brothers were excited to see their cousin again and hoped he'd stay, offering him a job at the ranch.

The party was also a celebration of sorts for the entire family. After months and months of financial and emotional struggle in the wake of former patriarch August Dempsey's death, the ranch was finally on the road to recovery. Not to mention Cole and Violet's recent elopement and Josh and Cara's engagement. Gabe and Reese were likely headed for the altar as well, though no formal announcement had yet been made.

For those reasons and more, Summer felt obligated to attend. She briefly considered leaving Teddy at home with his regular sitter. The party was scheduled to start at six— she could leave by eight, no problem. But the Dempsey brothers, along with Gabe's mother, Raquel, the family's well-loved matriarch, had insisted Summer bring Teddy. Besides, Josh's two children were also going to be there.

Summer had relented, of course, though other children at the party would make no difference. Teddy didn't socialize. With *anyone*. Children or adults or even his own mother.

A man appeared behind Summer, materializing in her peripheral vision. She assessed him instantly, something she'd learned to do out of necessity. He was young, maybe early thirties. Possibly a ranch hand, given his clothes, though, he didn't look familiar and Summer knew, or knew of, most everyone in their small community.

Whoever he was, he seemed concerned about nothing more than finding the correct aisle for whatever purchases he was making and promptly wandered off. Good thing, because Teddy had started humming, something he did to calm himself when he became nervous or agitated.

"Well, big guy." Summer smiled down at him. "Let's find the vanilla extract and get out of here."

The other ingredients were already nestled in Teddy's lap. He'd insisted on holding them.

Summer pushed her cart forward, being exceedingly careful not to touch Teddy. He tolerated contact better now than he used to, thanks to the learning center he was enrolled in and his weekly equine therapy sessions. Still, he picked and chose his moments. Summer could never be sure.

Suddenly two grandmotherly women rounded the corner and started down the aisle toward Summer and Teddy. She froze, halting the cart in midstep. The women were also strangers, likely passing through Mustang Valley on their way to or from Payson. Travelers regularly stopped at the market for refreshments.

Don't talk to us, please. The words were a mantra inside Summer's head.

Stare. Make judgments. Gossip about us later in your car. I don't care. Just please, please, please don't talk to us.

The woman on the left smiled and nodded. In another minute, possibly less, they would be upon Summer and Teddy and want to pass by.

Summer's grip on the cart handle tightened until her fingers cramped and her knuckles turned white.

Turn around now. Leave us alone.

Surrendering to the pressure building inside her, she

started walking backward, taking the cart with her. Hopefully, Teddy hadn't seen the women. They were behind him, after all.

No such luck. His humming grew louder, and he started banging the heels of his sneakers on the bottom of the cart basket, a sure indicator he'd noticed the women.

Summer moved faster. Glancing back over her shoulder, she spotted Dennis, the store manager. He'd be no help, and besides, Teddy made him uncomfortable.

"I think the vanilla extract's in the next aisle," she said cheerfully, knowing full well it wasn't.

All at once, the two women increased their strides, reaching Summer and Teddy before they made good on their escape.

The smiling one said, "Do you by chance know where the aspirin is?"

"Front of the store," Summer said. *Go away.*

Sweat dampened her palms and collected between her breasts. She could feel rivulets forming at her temples.

"Thank you." It looked as if the two women might turn around.

Before Summer could release even the tiniest sigh of relief, the one on the left stepped to the side of Summer's cart and looked directly at Teddy.

"Hi there, young man. How are you today?"

He averted his face and cringed, his rocking and humming gaining momentum. The tune wasn't distinct, rather he repeated the same five notes over and over.

Bang, bang, bang. His heels hit the cart basket harder and harder.

"He's kind of old to ride in a cart, isn't he?" The woman's tone left no doubt of her opinion. "What are you, son? Eight? Nine?"

"Have a good day." Summer resumed walking backward, intent only on getting to the one open register and escaping the store before Teddy lost control.

"I'm sorry. My sister didn't mean anything." The first woman caught up with Summer, her expression going from concern to suspicion. "Are you okay, young man? Is something the matter?"

Before Summer reached the end of the aisle, what she'd been dreading most happened. The woman reached out and touched Teddy, her hand resting on his shoulder.

"Young man?"

His reaction was instantaneous and, at this point, unstoppable. Ear-splitting shrieks erupted and filled the small market. His rocking turned into thrashing. One by one, he threw the items from his lap onto the floor.

Summer reacted without thinking, having experienced this same outburst countless times and as recently as last week. Reaching the open area near the front of the market, she swiveled the cart one hundred and eighty degrees and ran it toward the entrance. The double doors swooshed open in the nick of time. She and Teddy burst outside into the bright July sunshine.

"Miss! Miss." The woman ran after them.

Summer hurried. Very little time remained before Teddy passed the point of no return and hurt himself or Summer.

The cart bumped wildly as she ran it over the uneven asphalt. Fumbling for her purse at her side, she dug her keys out and pressed the button on the fob that unlocked the car.

As Teddy's screeching escalated—she hadn't thought it possible—she wrenched open the rear passenger door. Keeping one eye glued on him, she grabbed a large black cowboy hat off the floor. So far, so good. He wasn't trying to climb out of the cart.

Anticipating what lay ahead, she drew in a deep breath,

steeled her resolve and took hold of Teddy by the waist. Lifting him out of the cart, she quickly deposited him in the booster car seat.

He lost all control, screaming, kicking the back of the driver's seat and clawing at her. Trying to contain him with one arm, she plunked the hat on his head. At first, he pushed it off but allowed her second attempt. When the brim fell over his eyes and shrouded him in darkness, he began to quiet.

"Miss? Can I help?"

"We're all right. Thank you," Summer said firmly. She didn't look at the woman and focused her attention entirely on Teddy.

"Is there someone I can call?"

Like 9-1-1 to report her for abusing her child? It had happened before.

Teddy's shrieks and thrashing resumed.

"We're okay. Really." Summer tried reasoning with the woman. "My son is easily upset by strangers."

Can you not see he's special-needs? Do I have to say autistic?

"Okay," the woman muttered. "If you're sure."

She left—thank God. Summer lowered her head until it was level with Teddy's and began singing a childhood rhyme in a soft voice.

"The eensie, weensie spider went up the water spout. Down came the rain and washed the spider out."

He hummed and rocked in rhythm to the melody.

"Up came the sun, and it dried up all the rain. And the eensie, weensie spider went up the spout again."

Two more times she sang the song. Then, taking a chance, she inched a hand closer and buckled him into his booster seat. Next, she slipped away and started the car, turning the air-conditioning on high. July in Arizona could be counted on for hundred-plus degree temperatures. Teddy, however, seemed impervious to the heat.

In colder weather, she used a quilt to calm her son. He preferred the weight and volume over the lightness of a cowboy hat, but in this heat, he'd smother, so she improvised.

"Better now, sweetie pie?" She returned to her position next to him, careful to avoid contact.

He shook his head, the oversize hat flopping. But he seemed to have relaxed so she decided he must be improved.

"Excuse me, ma'am." A deep male voice interrupted her. "You left your groceries."

She rose and pivoted, emitting a small gasp at the sight of the cowboy from the market standing so close to her. He held out a plastic grocery sack.

"Wh-what?"

"Your groceries. You forgot them."

She shook her head in confusion. "I didn't buy them."

"It's okay." He shrugged.

"Did you pay for these?"

Behind Summer, Teddy shifted. He could hear the man even if he couldn't see him from under the hat's wide brim. She prayed that he didn't have another meltdown.

"Don't worry about it," the man said. "I could see you were…in a hurry." Not a trace of reproach or disapproval or shock colored his deep voice.

She blinked, then stared. Who was he?

"Look," she began to explain. "It's not what you think."

"I don't think anything, ma'am. It's none of my business."

Still, she felt the need to explain. The man had been kind, unlike the women who'd been curious and interfering. "My son is autistic and struggles in social situations."

In her support group, she was encouraged not to make excuses for her son. If people didn't understand, or if they poked fun at her and Teddy, well, that was their problem. Not hers. Still, it wasn't easy.

"I understand. I struggle myself at times." There was an honesty in his statement that took her momentarily aback.

He was handsome. Handsome enough that if Summer wasn't preoccupied with her son, she'd be intrigued. Brown eyes with flecks of gold studied her intently. Broad shoulders and muscled arms emphasized the snug fit of his black T-shirt. Scuffed cowboy boots added an inch to his already impressive height. Stubble darkened his strong jawline. That, along with a noticeable scar beside his left eye, lent a mysterious, if not dangerous, element to his looks.

"Let me pay you." Summer reached for her purse, which she'd left on the ground.

"It's not necessary."

"Yes, it is," she insisted as she handed him several bills.

He hesitated before accepting. Stuffing the money in his jeans pocket, he tugged on the brim of his hat.

"See you around."

Would he? She almost hoped that were true. After a moment, she came to her senses. Summer didn't date. Ever. Not that she wouldn't enjoy being in a relationship. But she and Teddy were a package deal. It wasn't easy finding an understanding and patient guy who'd accept and love a boy who wasn't his. Finding a guy who'd accept and love a special-needs child who wasn't his was nearly impossible.

"Thank you again," she said.

He seemed almost disappointed, as if he'd expected her to ask him to stay. Before she could say another word, he turned and left, disappearing into the store.

Summer stood and watched him go, the grocery sack growing heavy in her hand.

"Maw Maw."

Teddy calling her by name. He was definitely feeling better.

"Let's go home, honey. What do you say?"

She slowly removed the cowboy hat and laid it on the car floor. Getting behind the wheel, she pulled out of the parking lot. There was still time to make the cookies before the party.

"Man," Teddy said from the rear seat. "Wide haws."

"That's right. The man was a cowboy and rides horses."

Her thoughts drifted to him. She recalled his strong, compelling features. His kindness. The scar by his eye— surely there was a story there. Not that it mattered, but it was too bad she'd forgotten to introduce herself. Neither had she gotten his name.

Only when she reached her driveway did she realize she'd also forgotten the vanilla extract.

THREE DAYS AT Dos Estrellas Ranch, and Quinn Crenshaw felt as if he'd been living there for months. No, that wasn't entirely accurate. He felt as if he was home, in a way he hadn't felt at home for a long, long time.

The hammer rested easily in his hand, fitting perfectly in the crook of his palm. Raising it, he brought the head down hard on the nail, enjoying the loud *thwang* and the reverberation running up the length of his arm.

This was good work. Real work. Meaningful work. He'd missed it during the last two years, three months and fourteen days. For the majority of that time, he'd labored as a janitor, earning pennies an hour. Prisoner wages. Most of it was spent in the commissary. The remainder of his savings, thirty-two dollars and change, had been given to him when he was released six weeks ago.

His parents had funded his trip to Mustang Valley.

Without their help, he couldn't have afforded the gas for the fourteen-hour drive and the new tires his six-year-old pickup had desperately needed. Nor would he have had the cash to purchase the woman's groceries earlier today at the market. He hadn't wanted to take her money, but he could see it was important for her to repay him.

She was pretty, and he hadn't been able to stop thinking about her since their encounter. Freckles were his undoing, and the small sprinkling across her nose and cheeks was the perfect amount. She also appeared devoted to her son and was dealing with difficult circumstances to the best of her abilities.

Both were qualities Quinn admired and appreciated. His parents hadn't wavered once in their support of him during his arrest, trial and imprisonment.

Granted, he was reading a lot into a brief meeting and could be coming to a wrong conclusion. Quinn would bet, however, that he was right about the woman. Too bad he'd likely never see her again. And if he did see her, he was hardly in a position to pursue more than a casual acquaintance. He was innocent of any crime and completely exonerated thanks to new evidence. That didn't change the fact he was an ex-con with a record, one not cleared yet.

She'd said her son was autistic. Quinn had heard of the disorder, but his knowledge ended there. He might learn more while at Dos Estrellas. The equine therapy program that operated at the ranch currently had over thirty special-needs children enrolled, some coming from as far away as Scottsdale, Fountain Hills and Phoenix. Cara had told him as much yesterday. She was his cousin Josh's fiancée and the head of the therapy program. Quinn would be one of the groomsmen in their wedding next month.

"What are you doing, mister?"

Hearing a child's voice, Quinn straightened. He'd been

bent over the wooden arena post, repairing a loose railing, and hadn't heard the girl and horse approach.

"Fixing this." He pointed at the railing with his hammer.

"Why?" She spoke with a pronounced lisp.

"It was loose. Now it's not."

The girl, an adorable pixie, giggled impishly from where she sat atop a brown mare. Ten or twelve—he wasn't good at judging ages—her distinctive almond-shaped eyes narrowed to small slits as her smile widened.

Quinn grinned in return, something he rarely did. The girl was responsible. Children were open and much more accepting than adults. He could relax around them.

What did his daughter look and act like? Was she cute and bubbly or shy and quiet? The questions plagued Quinn constantly and angered him on those nights when sleep eluded him. The private investigator he'd hired hadn't located his daughter or her mother, claiming they'd gone into deep hiding. Quinn couldn't disagree. His own efforts had failed to produce results.

Running out of money, he'd let the PI go after only a week. Until one of the feelers he'd put out netted results or he landed a job that paid more than room and board, his search had come to a grinding halt.

"Is that a scar on your face?" The young girl pushed at her pink riding helmet, which had slipped low on her brow. A harness secured her to the saddle, preventing her from falling off.

"Yep."

"How did you get it?" she asked.

"An accident."

A fellow inmate's fist had "accidentally" struck Quinn's face during a fight his first week in the California state prison when he'd refused to give up his place in the cafeteria line. He'd spent two days in the infirmary with a mild concussion, three cracked ribs, multiple contusions and a dozen stitches.

Quinn learned fast. The fight wasn't his last one, but it was the last one he lost. Twenty-seven months in all had been added to his sentence. Fortunately, he hadn't had to serve them.

"Lizzie." The instructor rushed over to the girl. The brown mare, well trained, did no more than bob her head. "I told you not to ride off."

A group of six students had been practicing at the other end of the arena.

"Sorry." Lizzie smiled at Quinn before turning a contrite face to her instructor. "I didn't hear you."

"You know the rules." The instructor took hold of the horse's bridle. "No riding off and no talking to strangers."

"He's not a stranger. He works here. He's fixing the loose railing."

"Come on." The instructor was having none of it. She led the pair away, her scowl telegraphing her thoughts loud and clear. She didn't want the students having anything to do with Quinn. He supposed she'd heard about him. News traveled fast, titillating news that much faster.

Lizzie ignored her instructor and, glancing backward, waved at Quinn. He raised his hand in return, then let it drop.

Moments like this one never lasted. Maybe someday, if he was lucky, his life would return to normal and his daughter would be a large part of it. He wasn't holding his breath.

"Somehow I knew I'd find you here."

He spun to discover his cousin Josh standing there, Cara with him. Both of them were staring.

"Where else would I be? You said the arena railing had

come loose." Quinn didn't wait around to be told what to do next. Rather, he took it upon himself to handle the task.

"You might be getting ready for the party," Josh said. "It starts in an hour."

Only then did Quinn notice the two of them were dressed up. "Plenty of time."

Cara hitched her chin toward the end of the arena where Lizzie and the students were completing their session. "Admit it. You like watching the kids."

"Just familiarizing myself with the therapy program."

She didn't call him out on his partial fib. "Lizzie's pretty cute."

"A little Down syndrome doesn't hold her back."

"We saw you with her earlier. You were great. You're going to do well here." Cara nudged Josh.

He nodded in agreement. "Yeah, you are."

"We'll see." If Quinn had learned one thing in the last three years, it was to not presume anything.

"Cara and I were thinking." Josh spoke somberly while his fiancée struggled to contain her excitement. "If you're agreeable—"

She cut him off. "Between the wedding and a baby on the way, I need help with the mustang sanctuary and therapy program. I—we—want you to be the one." When Quinn didn't immediately respond, she said, "We're offering you a job."

He dropped the hammer in the toolbox at his feet, buying himself a few seconds while the shock wore off.

"I thought you hired me as a ranch hand."

"Divide your days," Josh said. "Mornings, the therapy program and sanctuary. Afternoons, cattle ranching."

"I'm not qualified to work with kids."

Cara dismissed him with a laugh. "I don't need help with the kids. I need someone to oversee the horses. You're a ten-time national rodeo champion. I think that qualifies you."

"How do you know you can trust me? You just met me the other day."

"I'm a good judge of character." She surprised him again by reaching for his hand and clasping it between hers. "Please say yes. The job comes with a small salary, and I emphasize small. The therapy program is still in the beginning stages. Eventually, there might be an increase."

She didn't say it, but she clearly understood that Quinn needed money to rehire the private investigator.

Josh, too, apparently, for he added, "Eventually, Cole, Gabe and I hope to pay you. As soon as the ranch is turning a decent profit again. And we're close."

"I'm grateful for what you've done."

"We need you," Cara said. "*I* need you."

Quinn studied her, searching for any sign of insincerity. He saw none. "For the record, I realize I'm not the kind of person who inspires faith."

"You're wrong, Quinn," she said.

"Can I think about it for a day?"

"Take all the time you need," Josh said.

"Tomorrow will be fine," Cara added brightly.

Quinn grabbed the toolbox. He did need a shower and shave before the party. "I'd better get a move on."

Josh and Cara left, heading for the house. Her satisfied smile was hard to miss. Did she assume he'd accept her job offer? If she did, she had good reason.

Quinn chuckled to himself as he returned the toolbox to the shed behind the horse stables. He'd just been had by someone skilled, and he didn't mind. In fact, he liked it.

Forty minutes later on the dot, he left the tiny apartment over the stables where he bunked. Boots shined and wearing clean clothes, he walked into the living room at the ranch house and faced a roomful of people. Many of them were from neighboring cattle ranches. They might be the Dempseys' competitors, but they were also good friends, having known August and Raquel for decades.

Quinn's cousins, Josh and Cole, came forward to greet him, clapping his back and pulling him into friendly hugs. Their half brother, Gabe, was next. Though no relation, he treated Quinn like a cousin. There were more guests, a couple dozen at least. Quinn met each one but quickly began forgetting names.

He was conversing with Cara and Theo McGraw, the Dempseys' neighbor and Gabe's future father-in-law, when a pretty woman with freckles and strawberry blond hair entered the room. Quinn caught sight of her, and time came to an abrupt halt. It started up again when she met his gaze, a startled expression on her lovely face.

Her son accompanied her, hovering close to her side, and was much calmer than this morning.

"Look," Cara exclaimed. "There's Summer and Teddy. She's my best friend and maid of honor at the wedding."

Summer, like the season. Quinn decided the name suited her. She was bright as sunshine and vivid blue skies. Appealing as long, carefree days that stretched into warm, endless evenings.

Suddenly, he wanted to meet her. Officially. "Introduce us."

"Good idea," Cara said. "You'll be spending a lot of time together, what with all the pre-wedding hoopla."

Quinn wasn't unhappy at the prospect despite the fact he had no business "spending time together," as Cara had put it.

As they neared, Summer's eyes widened, and he swore he could see her mind putting the pieces together. He wasn't just the man she'd met earlier at the market, he was the guest of honor. Why else would Cara be escorting him over?

"Summer, I want you to meet Quinn Crenshaw."

Cara might have surprised him with a job offer, but he had an even bigger surprise in store for her.

"We've met," Quinn said.

Summer swallowed, then smiled tentatively in return. "Yes. Earlier today at the market. Except we each didn't realize who the other person was."

"Oh!" Cara drew back to study each of them. "Really?"

"He helped me with Teddy." Summer extended her hand. "It's nice to meet you, Quinn."

"Same here." He closed his fingers around her slim and deceptively strong ones, lingered for too long, then turned his attention to Teddy rather than give himself away. "How you doing, son?"

The boy peered up at him but didn't meet Quinn's gaze. He noticed Teddy favored his mother. Same color hair, same freckles and same hazel eyes.

"We're doing much better," Summer answered for him. "Shopping can sometimes be stressful. Thank you again."

"My pleasure." Quinn meant it.

Cara blinked in astonishment, taking the three of them in. "I really wish I'd been there. This sounds interesting."

"Truly, it wasn't." Summer smiled somberly. "A woman touched Teddy, and, well, you know how he hates that. Quinn was kind and helped me out."

"Man," Teddy suddenly said. "Stow."

"That's right." Summer beamed. "Mr. Crenshaw is the man we met at the store."

Cara also seemed impressed. "Wow. He's really talking more and more."

"Between the learning center and the therapy program, he's making incredible strides." They chatted for several more minutes until Cara was called away to help with dinner. Summer smoothly changed the subject. "Quinn, I hear you're a rodeo champion."

At least she hadn't said *ex-convict*. "Former champion."

"Bull riding?"

"That was Josh and Cole's event, though I did give it a go now and then. Mostly then. Bronc busting, bareback and saddle was my choice of torture, along with a little steer wrestling."

"Torture?"

She glanced down at her son again, who continued to stare at Quinn's left ear. It should have made him uncomfortable. For whatever reason, it didn't.

"Rodeoing isn't exactly easy." But it was a hell of a lot easier than prison.

"Do you miss it?"

"Every day." Quinn wasn't sure why he felt compelled to be so forthright with Summer.

"I hear you're taking to cattle ranching. Josh says you're a natural."

"Cara offered me a job. Helping with the mustangs and the therapy program."

Summer's mouth opened, then shut and thinned to a flat line. Whatever she was going to say, she'd changed her mind.

Her reaction bothered him. "Don't feel you have to stay and keep me company."

"Sorry." Her denial was quick and not quite believable. "I should probably help with dinner, too. I don't want to leave everything to Cara and Raquel."

"Sure." His ready acquiescence wasn't entirely believable, either. Not to his ears anyway. Apparently not to Summer's, either.

For the first time she faltered. "I… It's not…"

"Is there a problem with me working for Cara?"

"No. What gave you that idea?"

"Because you changed the second I mentioned it."

"I think it's a wonderful opportunity." When Cara called her name, she couldn't escape fast enough. "Excuse me." Checking on her son, she let out a soft, "Oh."

Quinn felt it then. Teddy was tracing his index finger along the engraving on his leather belt depicting a herd of galloping horses.

"Hey, son."

"Haws. Wunning."

"Yes, the horses are running." Summer blinked back tears.

Quinn issued the invitation without thinking. "He can stay with me if he wants."

"No." She shook her head vehemently, her tears instantly drying. "No," she repeated, starting for the kitchen. Except Teddy didn't follow her. "Come on, honey."

He stuck out his lower lip, his concentration focused on his finger as it traveled from one horse to the other on Quinn's belt.

Summer wavered, visibly torn.

"I have a solution," Quinn said amicably. "I'll go with you and Teddy."

Again Summer shook her head in protest. But when Quinn started walking, Teddy did, too.

Chapter Two

Quinn had been to Arizona many times during the years he competed. There were several well-known rodeos in the state, the Parada del Sol being one of the biggest and most popular. He'd heard of Mustang Valley from his cousins, mostly how they'd refused to set foot in the place again after what they viewed as their father's abandonment, but he hadn't visited.

Then their father's death had brought them home after a long, long absence. In a way, it had also brought Quinn there.

He stared at the distant outline of the McDowell Mountains, grateful for his recent good fortune. This was a place worth living in and not just because he'd spent the last two-plus years calling a stark concrete cell the size of a closet home.

Dusk fell, and the sun disappeared behind the horizon, leaving behind a half moon hovering above Pinnacle Peak. A flock of doves took flight from a nearby paloverde tree and winged their way into the great expanse of the desert. Distant lowing from some of Dos Estrellas' twelve hundred head of cattle grew softer and less frequent as they settled in for the night.

Quinn stood in the front courtyard of the Dempsey house. Behind the ranch and a good two miles north lay the town. In this direction, however, the land seemed to extend forever.

Inside the house, the party continued strong. He'd escaped after dinner and come outside, hoping no one was offended. His need for solitude wasn't the fault of the guests. They were all nice and cheerfully welcomed him, though some couldn't hide their curiosity.

He simply liked being alone and shutting out all the noise until only his own thoughts remained. At times the craving was too powerful to resist, and he gave in.

That might be the reason he liked and understood Teddy. Sometimes a person didn't want to be touched or talked to or bothered.

Quinn thought Summer must also understand Teddy. At least, she tried. She certainly respected his boundaries.

He compared his own situation to Summer's, noting the differences. He'd been denied the chance to parent his daughter and longed for contact with her. Summer, however, lived with Teddy but wasn't allowed to touch him. How hard that must be for her.

An exterior light came on. The next instant, the front door to the house, a large and ornately engraved oak panel, swung open. Summer stepped outside as if by thinking of her Quinn had made her appear. Teddy, as usual, stood beside her.

She obviously hadn't seen Quinn yet and assumed she had the courtyard to herself. He would have relished the chance to observe her unnoticed, except in the next instant Josh's two young children tumbled outside like a pair of puppies set free after being confined all day.

Nathan, Josh's three-year-old son, bounded over to where Quinn sat on the stone bench by the fountain. "Hi, Uncle Quinn. What are you doing?"

The boy had started calling him "Uncle" without any

encouragement. While technically inaccurate, Quinn didn't mind.

"Nothing much. What about you?"

"Daddy says I'm being bad. Too noisy."

The boy was followed by his ever-present shadow, his eighteen-month-old sister, Kimberly. She babbled in a baby language Quinn couldn't translate.

His throat strangely tightened. His daughter—hell, he didn't even know her name—was maybe six months younger than Nathan. He didn't know her exact age, either. Damn. It wasn't fair. Frustration built before he could contain it.

"I'm sorry. We didn't mean to disturb you."

Hearing Summer's voice, he glanced up to see her and Teddy approach.

"No problem," Quinn answered. "It's a beautiful evening. A shame not to enjoy it."

"Those two were being a bit rambunctious. I offered to take them outside. Teddy needed a break anyway."

Quinn angled his head to better see Teddy. "I know how you feel, pal. Crowds get to me, too."

The boy rewarded Quinn by making eye contact for a few seconds.

"He likes you," Summer said, a trace of wonder in her voice.

"The feeling's mutual."

"Noooo," Kimberly abruptly cried out, her one understandable word. Frowning, she pushed at Nathan.

He retaliated by kneeling in front of the fountain, dipping his hand in the tepid water and splashing her. She screamed as if doused with boiling lava.

Quinn stood. Before he could intervene, Summer did.

"Hey, you two. Behave."

"She hit me," Nathan objected, scrambling to his feet.

"You're bigger and older than her."

She attempted to reason with the boy, explaining how it was his job to set a good example for his sister. From the way Nathan stuck out his lower lip, Quinn could see he wasn't taking the lesson to heart. Beside him, Teddy began humming. Quinn didn't think it bode well.

Something he hadn't thought of in years suddenly popped into his head. Reaching for his wallet, he extracted a dollar bill. Teddy watched Quinn's every move as he executed a number of intricate folds. Before too long, the bill resembled a swan. A rather crooked swan, mind you. Quinn's skills were rusty.

"Here. Take it." He handed the swan to Teddy.

After lengthy and careful consideration, Teddy took it.

"Come on." Quinn walked to the fountain, motioning to Teddy.

The boy just stared, his eyes void of expression.

Quinn pointed to the water. "Swans like to swim."

By now, Summer, Nathan and even Kimberly watched in fascination.

Finally Teddy complied. At the fountain's edge, he gingerly set the paper swan on the water. It bobbed gently and floated toward the center of the fountain.

"I want one, too." Nathan rushed Quinn and hugged his thigh.

"You have to be good."

"I will. I be good."

Quinn quickly constructed a second swan. Nathan smashed its tail before launching it in the water. He didn't appear to mind. Kimberly eagerly squeezed between the boys. Teddy remained rooted to his spot, ignoring both other children.

Summer sidled up beside Quinn. "Where did you learn to make those?"

"My sister. She was into origami for a while when we were kids. I can also make an eagle and a ring. Or, I could. Maybe not now."

"A man of many talents."

He liked the silky quality of her voice and the fluid grace of her movements. "I'd forgotten about it until now."

"Memories are funny things. They can be buried for years and surface all at once. Then there are those that are never far away."

Quinn had a lot of those kind.

By unspoken agreement, they moved to the bench, where they could keep the children in sight. It wasn't a large bench, and only a few inches separated them. Aided by the exterior light that had come on automatically, Quinn saw a tiny jeweled stud in her right ear, appreciated her attractive profile and discerned at least three distinct shades of color in her hair, ranging from blond to gold to red.

He shouldn't ask but he did anyway. "Is Teddy's dad in the picture? I noticed you came to the party alone."

"He is." Summer shrugged. "Barely."

"A shame."

"I agree. Teddy was three when the doctors officially diagnosed him. By then, our quiet but seemingly happy child had almost completely withdrawn and barely spoke. Hal didn't take the diagnosis well. Up until then, he hoped whatever was wrong with Teddy was treatable and reversible. We divorced about a year later. He was visiting every few months." Her voice altered slightly. "He remarried this past winter. Since then, he's been coming by every couple of weeks. I think his new wife has more to do with it than any sense of responsibility."

Quinn chose to keep his opinion of Summer's ex to himself.

She gave an embarrassed laugh. "I can't believe I told you all that. We barely know each other."

"Sometimes it's easier to talk to strangers."

"Teddy doesn't seem to notice the lack of a father in his life. Truthfully, he's been more aware of you in the last fifteen minutes than of Hal in the past year." She stared into the distance.

Quinn wondered if she saw the same beauty and majesty he had earlier or if she took it for granted. He liked to think the former. Summer struck him as a sensitive person.

She cleared her throat. "I owe you an apology."

"For what?"

"I was wrong earlier. You should accept the job. You'll be wonderful. With the horses *and* the children."

"You have good reason to be worried. I spent over two years in prison."

"I wasn't worried."

"To have doubts, then."

She glanced at the children. Teddy continued to focus on the paper swans, now becoming waterlogged. The younger two had abandoned the fountain to play with a tennis ball they'd found in a bush.

"Josh and Cole told me you're innocent. That new evidence cleared you."

"I didn't hurt the guy. But we did get into an altercation that night in the bar. There was some shoving. Shouting. Threats. I'd like to say he had it coming. Truthfully, I've had…problems with my temper in the past. Still do."

"You're kidding. You strike me as pretty laid-back."

"Ah. Well, I work on it. Constantly. Prison's good for changing a person's perspective. Maybe the only thing it's good for."

"You didn't let it destroy you, Quinn. That's what's important."

She was wrong. Prison had destroyed a part of him he could never get back. The part that had fearlessly faced life.

"The guy was a jerk." Quinn had called him far worse names when not in earshot of kids.

"What did he do that made you angry?" she asked. "Besides being a jerk. Hit on your girlfriend?"

"Yes."

She drew back. "I wasn't serious."

"He insulted her. And when I say insult, I'm being generous. We'd both had a lot to drink. The difference was, I'd just come off a big win while he'd lost. My friends separated us and got me out of the bar, then took me to my truck. The guy left the bar a while later and was assaulted in the parking lot. He nearly died from a brain hemorrhage and was in a coma for weeks. When he finally regained consciousness, he identified me as his assailant even though the attack happened so fast he didn't see the guy's face."

"Why would he do that?"

"A blue shirt. I was wearing one. And apparently his assailant was, too."

"Are you saying you were arrested and convicted based on the fact you were wearing a blue shirt? I don't believe it."

"More than a dozen people witnessed our argument in the bar."

"But not the attack. Didn't you have an alibi? What about your friends? Your girlfriend? Surely they vouched for you."

"They couldn't. After they left me at my truck, they went home or back to their hotel rooms, including Jenny. She was mad. She'd grown pretty tired of me by that point. I crawled into the backseat and went to sleep. No one saw me until the next morning."

"What about security cameras? Weren't there any?"

"Only one and it had been broken for months. The bar owner hadn't gotten around to fixing it."

She shook her head. "This sounds like a bad TV show."

"My guilt was proven beyond a shadow of a doubt in the minds of the jurors."

"Doesn't that make you mad?"

"Yes, it did. Really mad. I had a lot of trouble controlling my rage the first six months in prison. Counseling helped. Now that I'm out, I try not to dwell on the past. It doesn't do any good."

"What happened? How were you exonerated?" Summer leaned in.

Quinn did, too, finding her proximity impossible to resist. "DNA evidence. None of mine was at the scene, which didn't make a difference to the jurors. But there was blood not belonging to me or the guy on his clothing. He must have gotten in a swing at some point. Problem was no match was found in the federal DNA database. Six months ago, I caught a break when the real assailant was arrested for another unrelated assault. This time, the victim was his wife."

Summer gasped.

"She told the police her husband had a history of violence and was involved in several bar fights. The police were able to match his DNA to the sample from the guy's shirt. It took a while, but I was cleared and the right man put in prison."

"I'm really glad, Quinn."

"Yeah." He blew out a long breath. Did she have to look at him so earnestly and with such compassion? "There's more." He hesitated. "I have a daughter."

"You do?" She brightened. "Where does she live? How old is she? Is she going to visit?"

He smiled. Next to kids, she more than anyone could coax one out of him. "I don't have the answer to any of those questions. I've never seen her. I only just found out about her. A friend of Jenny's told me after I got released. She thought I should know."

"Jenny hid your daughter from you?"

"I don't blame her. I'm a convict."

"Was. The girl is your daughter. You have rights."

"I've been trying to find them. I even hired a private investigator."

"Any luck?"

"Not yet. I need this job. PIs aren't cheap."

Summer looked stricken. "Now I'm even sorrier about earlier."

"Don't sweat it."

She surprised him by saying, "I might be able to help you."

"You can?" He didn't see how.

"I work part-time for an attorney in Scottsdale. He specializes in family law. We occasionally have to track down errant spouses, some of whom have taken their children."

"I can't afford an attorney, either." Quinn had already gone that route.

"He might talk to you pro bono. Offer some free advice. Let me ask," she said when he hesitated. "What harm can it do? You may be able to receive compensation from the state."

"Sue them?"

"You were falsely imprisoned. They may offer a settlement. In fact, I'm surprised they didn't already. It's worth checking into."

Pride and hope waged a battle inside Quinn. He didn't like taking handouts. Then again, he'd be a fool to refuse help and possibly money when he desperately needed both. "Okay."

By some miracle, Nathan and Kimberly continued to play without fighting. Teddy stayed put by the fountain, absorbed in his own world.

Feeling Summer's warm hand on his arm, Quinn turned.

"I'm glad you told me about everything," she said. "It couldn't have been easy."

She looked directly at him with those enormous hazel eyes, and Quinn felt a small crack form in the shield protecting his damaged heart. He stood before the crack had a chance to widen.

"We should probably get back to the party." He went over and collected his niece and nephew, ignoring the confusion clouding Summer's features.

She was exactly the kind of woman he could fall for. Unfortunately, he was exactly the kind of man she should avoid at all costs. If she didn't realize it, he certainly did and would avoid any involvement for both their sakes.

THERE WERE CURRENTLY six therapy-program horses being housed in the row of covered stalls behind the horse stables, all of them rehabilitated mustangs from the sanctuary Cara ran. In addition to the stalls, the program had also built the small riding arena where Quinn met Lizzie.

The nearby corral was sometimes reserved for private lessons when a more confined area was needed. On most days, Cole used it to train horses. With two hundred wild mustangs to rehabilitate and adopt out, training had quickly become his specialty and main job at the ranch. Quinn was lucky to find the corral empty.

Deciding to familiarize himself with his new charges, he led all six horses from their stalls to the corral. Normally, controlling this many horses at one time was difficult. But the well-trained and quiet-natured group obediently followed behind the mare Quinn held by a lead rope. At the corral, the horses stood and waited until he opened the gate.

Unhooking the rope, he clucked to the mare and patted her chunky hind end. The other five horses followed through the gate, needing very little encouragement from Quinn. Once inside, they came to a stop and either nosed the ground or stood at the corral railing, snorting and swishing their tails.

Two days working for the therapy program and Quinn had already learned a lot about the ins and outs. This time of year, because of the warm temperatures, students scheduled their lessons either early in the morning, finishing by nine, or in the evenings, starting at six thirty when it was less hot.

Just last week, a floodlight had been installed to aid the evening lessons. While the remainder of Dos Estrellas Ranch rested after a long day, the therapy program operated in full force. None of the Dempseys were there, with the occasional exception of Josh, who showed up because of Cara. Mostly, he stayed home to watch the kids.

He'd been there last night when Quinn arrived to observe the class, joining Cara while she advised Quinn on how the program worked. There'd been five students, two instructors, three volunteer helpers, one administrator, and five sets of parents. Summer and Teddy weren't among those gathered. Quinn admittedly looked for them despite his vow to keep his distance.

During the lesson, he'd made a point of observing the horses in action with the students and the program staff. Today he wanted to see how the horses acted without riders and a small crowd distracting them. He was specifically interested in any personality quirks that might interfere with performance or abilities being overlooked and underutilized.

He put the horses through their paces, getting them to trot and lope in a circle by swinging a lead rope in a circle over his head. The chunky brown mare named Mama was undeniably in charge. She might be a lamb when Lizzie or the other kids rode her but as far as preserving order among this small herd, Mama was a force to be reckoned with.

Within ten minutes, Quinn had made a number of important discoveries. Pancake and George Clooney didn't like to be separated and stuck together unless forced apart. Stargazer refused to lead with her left—though that might not be a problem as the students never loped the horses. Chubbs became agitated when approached from behind. Gidget's one flaw was a choppy gait. Then again, her rider last night had laughed when rocked from side to side.

Concerned most about Chubbs, Quinn examined him from nose to tail, expecting to find a sore hip or abscessed hoof. Something Chubbs felt the need to protect. What Quinn found gave him cause for concern. The old gelding wasn't entirely blind, but he did have some vision loss. That alone wouldn't drum him out of the therapy program, but the staff should be made aware and take necessary precautions.

None of the therapy horses were particularly good-looking. A couple were overweight, including Mama. On the positive side, they were a dependable, reliable and trustworthy lot. Perfect babysitters.

Quinn leaned his back against the corral railing. Sweat soaked his shirt, causing it to cling to his skin. Removing his cowboy hat, he knocked it against his leg to dislodge the dust.

What he'd give for a cold glass of water to quench his

parched throat. This was hot, hard work. Still, he wouldn't trade it for a million dollars. Quinn had considered returning to the rodeo circuit when he was first released. This was the better choice. Easing slowly into post-prison life made more sense than plowing full steam ahead without having any direction.

Turning, he caught sight of Cara, who, after yesterday, was officially his boss for the three to four hours a day he spent with the mustang sanctuary and therapy program. Closing the gate behind her, she wended her way toward him, petting a friendly nose here and there as the horses meandered over to greet her.

"A little warm to be out here," she said.

"I'm about done." He nodded at Chubbs. "Did you know he's partially blind?"

"I didn't." Cara evaluated the horse with crossed arms and a narrowed gaze. "Are you sure? He doesn't act blind."

"Haven't you noticed he dislikes being approached from behind?" Quinn demonstrated, using Mama.

"I have but I didn't associate it with partial blindness." Cara nodded approvingly. "How'd you know?"

"I had a blind donkey before. It's easy to overlook."

"You rode a donkey?"

"I *roped* a donkey. Easier to use them than calves when training a green roping horse. They don't spook like calves or tire as easily."

Quinn and Cara discussed the other program horses until she asked, "Is there any chance you can swing by the tuxedo rental store this week for your fitting? The wedding's going to be here before you know it."

"Sure. No problem."

"Thanks." Her eyes twinkled. Getting married looked good on her. On his cousin, too.

Quinn had grown up with both Josh and Cole back in

California. They were more like brothers, having lived in the same town and within miles of each other. But he'd always been a little closer to Josh. Seeing him about to get married to a great gal and become a father for the third time cheered Quinn, as did Cole's relationship with Violet. It made him believe there was still good in the world.

As far as Quinn was concerned, no one deserved to be happy more than his cousins. They'd suffered a lot, having a father who'd abandoned them at a young age and then being raised by a bitter, angry mother. Obtaining co-ownership of the ranch when August died last fall didn't make up for years of neglect.

Finding their future at Dos Estrellas did. It had changed them. Given them an entirely new outlook. Maybe the same would happen to Quinn.

Feeling his pocket vibrate, he plucked out his cell phone and frowned when he didn't recognize the number.

"Excuse me," he said to Cara, stepping away and answering. "Hello."

"Quinn? It's Summer. I hope you don't mind my calling. Cara gave me your number."

"No, it's all right." He glanced at Cara, who smiled guiltily. Apparently, she'd guessed the identity of his caller. "What's up?"

"I know it's short notice, but my boss had a cancellation this afternoon. He said he'd be glad to talk to you, if you can be here by four."

Was it a coincidence he got off work at three thirty?

Cara gave him a what-are-you-waiting-for wave, confirming his suspicions that she was in cahoots with Summer.

"Thanks, but I—"

"I'm sure Martin can help you," Summer insisted.

Quinn paused.

Her long sigh carried across the connection. "I'm being pushy, and I shouldn't. Finding your daughter is your business." She sighed again. "Sometimes I overstep. It's a bad habit."

He pictured her sitting at her desk, multitasking while they talked because she was probably a doer and a go-getter. His counselor in prison had been the same way. Except she wasn't nearly as pretty as Summer and was about thirty years older.

"Fine." He heard himself agreeing even before he'd decided. "See you at four. Can you text me the address?"

"Of course." She sounded surprised, then pleased. "I'll tell Martin. See you then."

Aware of Cara's stare, Quinn saved Summer's number to his contacts before clearing his screen, silently chiding himself while he did. What reason would he have to call her?

"You planned this," he said to Cara, acting madder than he was.

"I did give her your number when she told me why she wanted to call."

Quinn grabbed the lead rope from where he'd hung it on the corral post and hooked it to Mama's halter. Cara tagged along when he led the mare through the gate. As expected, the other five horses trailed behind them.

"Come on, Quinn." Cara squeezed past Mama. "She likes you, and I think you like her, too. In fact, I'm *sure* you like her."

Did being his cousin's fiancée automatically make Cara his friend? One with rights to butt into his personal business?

Quinn ground to a halt. The horses did, too, bumping into each other and jerking their heads back.

That was the problem with happy people. They wanted

everyone else to be happy, too, and went to great lengths to accomplish it.

"I'm not looking for a girlfriend, Cara. Besides, Summer can do a whole lot better than me."

"She's not like that. She accepts everyone for who they are. No judging."

Quinn didn't doubt it. Nonetheless, he said, "I don't want to hurt her."

"What makes you think you will?"

He groaned. "She needs someone who can step up. Be there for her and Teddy unconditionally and without hesitation. Someone who doesn't come with his own set of problems and can put them first. I'm not that man. And after what I've been through, I may never be him."

This time when he started for the stall, Cara didn't go with him. She stayed behind, apparently stunned into silence.

Chapter Three

Summer struggled to concentrate. Quinn was due any minute. He hadn't sounded enthused when she called earlier offering him the open appointment, but surely he'd show up. Finding his daughter was too important to him.

"What's with you today?" Her coworker Alicia plopped a stack of papers on her desk. In the years Summer had been employed with the small law firm, paralegals had come and gone. Alicia was one of the best.

"Nothing." Summer gave the stack a passing glance. They'd talked earlier about the copies and packages needing to be mailed before the end of the day.

"Could have fooled me. You've been on edge all afternoon. Is Teddy okay?"

"He's great. Improving every day and talking more and more."

Most important, there'd been no outbursts for almost a week, which had to be a record. She didn't count the battle they'd engaged in this morning over which shorts to wear or the one yesterday over lunch—she'd run out of peanut butter, an earth-shattering disaster. Those types of battles were par for the course as far as Summer was concerned. A regular part of their daily routine.

"Then what is it?" Alicia asked. She understood a lot of

what Summer had to deal with. Alicia cared for her ailing grandfather, whose senility continually worsened.

"Just a lot going on." Summer patted the stack. "I'd better get started on these."

A few minutes later, she gave a nervous start when the door to the office opened and Quinn strode in. He removed his hat with one hand, stopped when he spotted her behind the desk and nodded.

"Hey."

"Hi." She stood, automatically brushing the front of her slacks, though not a speck of lint dotted them. "Have a seat. I'll let Martin know you're here." She returned to her computer and opened a messaging window, sending her boss a quick alert. Seconds later, he responded. She read it out loud. "He'll be a few minutes."

"Thanks." Quinn picked one of the five empty visitor chairs in which to wait. He was their last appointment for the day.

Summer came out from behind her desk. "Can I get you a bottle of water or some coffee?"

"Water would be great, if you don't mind." He rested his cowboy hat on his lap, unable to look more uncomfortable if he tried.

She hurried to a nearby multipurpose room where a refrigerator was stored. It held a variety of beverages exclusively for clients. She grabbed the closest bottled water, decided it wasn't cold enough, replaced it and chose one farther back on the shelf.

"Seriously?" she asked herself as she took the cold bottle anyway. On the way back she nearly collided with Alicia. "Oops. Excuse me."

"Whoa, girl. Slow down. It's not as if he's going to spontaneously disappear on you."

"What? No. Don't be silly."

"Right." Alicia laughed, a full, rich sound. "And your all-fire hurry has nothing to do with that fine-looking man in the reception area and how you went into spasms the second he arrived."

"Spasms? I think I'm insulted." And impatient.

"Go on. Get outta here. I'll answer the phone if it rings."

"Humph." Summer, not nearly as put out as she pretended to be, pursed her lips and slipped past Alicia. By the time she reached Quinn in the waiting area, she wore a smile. "Here you go." Handing him the bottle—the cold bottle—she returned to her desk, which afforded her a nice, unobstructed view of him.

Checking her computer screen to make sure Martin hadn't contacted her during her short absence, she attacked the stack of documents Alicia had left on her desk.

"Thanks again for setting this up, Summer."

Hearing Quinn's voice, she glanced up. "Glad to do it."

"How's Teddy?"

"Good. He's in after-school daycare. I can't always coerce him into going. Today I got lucky. You may see him this evening. He has his equine therapy class. He hasn't actually ridden yet. Won't let anyone help him up into the saddle or put the harness on him. But he loves to pet and groom the horses and lead them around." She didn't add that Quinn might see her, too. She usually accompanied Teddy.

"I'll be sure to look for him."

"How's the new job going?" She should be working. Hadn't she promised Alicia the packages would be ready before five?

"I'm learning the ropes," he said. "Slowly but surely."

"Do you like it? That's the important part."

"Yeah. I do."

Quinn shifted nervously, his right boot softly tapping

the floor. He didn't look as though he'd spent a lot of hours in offices. Or, she suddenly realized, the hours he'd spent in them had been difficult to endure. Nothing fun about conferring with your defense attorney and fighting for your freedom.

"Cara's lucky to have you. You arrived in Mustang Valley at the perfect time."

"I did."

She'd meant that Cara needed assistance because the demands of her personal life had increased. The thoughtful quality in Quinn's tone implied something entirely different. She was even more curious about him than before.

Martin stepped in from the hall. "Mr. Crenshaw. It's nice to meet you."

Quinn stood. "Thank you for seeing me on such short notice."

The two men shook hands, and Martin invited Quinn into his office.

With nothing more to distract her, Summer quickly finished assembling the packages and then updated Martin's court calendar. She was more than a receptionist for the modest practice. In addition to managing the office, she handled all the billing and accounting. Martin was generous, allowing her to occasionally work from home by logging into her office computer remotely.

At about four forty-five, the office door abruptly opened. Summer stood at the lateral file and, hearing the sound, turned. Her heart immediately dropped to her knees.

"Hal. What are you doing here?" Her ex-husband was the last person she'd expected to see.

"I need to talk to you. It's about Teddy."

"You couldn't have just called me at home? You needed to ambush me at work?"

"This isn't an ambush."

Yet that was how it felt to Summer. He liked having the advantage, which taking her by surprise gave him, and frequently pulled stunts like this.

"You'll have to wait until I'm done." She turned her back on him, ready to resume her search for the files while also sending him a clear message.

"Dennis called me the other day."

The manager of the market? "Why would I care about that?"

"Because he told me Teddy had a tantrum and upset some of his customers."

Summer didn't take kindly to Hal's use of the word *tantrum*. And were the two women really that upset? She refrained from commenting for the moment and walked to her desk. "I left the store right away. It's not as if I enjoy making a scene."

"That's the point, Summer. According to Dennis, Teddy's had a bunch of tantrums in the market."

"A bunch? There's been maybe three."

"And how many has he had in other places you haven't told me about?"

"Outbursts are part of his disorder. You know that."

"Seems to me, he's been having more and more lately."

"That's not true." Summer's defenses instantly rose and, rather than insist he leave, she continued to engage him. A tiny voice warned her that was just what he wanted. "Teddy's been better behaved at home and the learning center than ever."

"Apparently not in public." Hal stood his ground. He was a handsome man, when he wasn't scowling. At the moment he stared at her with glinting eyes and a jutting jaw.

"Dr. Hamilton says Teddy's outbursts can be his way of exerting his independence or his frustration at communicating and not being understood."

"I'm not buying one bit of that."

"Right. Because you're such an authority on autism." Anger flared inside her. Hal could ignite it with a single remark. "You see Teddy barely more than a few hours a month. You're in no position to lecture me."

"It's just like you to overreact."

"Is that what I'm doing? You've refused to go with me to Teddy's doctor appointments or family counseling sessions for the last four years. You've never read even one of the books I bought."

"I've read plenty of books, Summer," he said with scorn.

"Ones Loren bought? Is she behind your sudden interest in Teddy?"

It was unfair of her to blame Hal's new wife, but ever since the two of them got married, Loren had been pushing him to take more of an interest in Teddy. They were trying to adopt, and it looked good on their application. Right thing, wrong reason, which was what bothered Summer. If not, she'd welcome Hal's and even Loren's interest in her son.

"Leave her out of this," he said, his voice increasing in volume. "And you need to start shopping someplace other than the market where everyone in town goes."

Where his buddy the manager worked, she almost spat out. Instead, she said, "I don't always have time to drive into Scottsdale for a few items."

"Obviously something about the market triggers Teddy's tantrums."

Summer had reached her boiling point. "You need to go, Hal. Now."

Alicia emerged from around the corner, a stern expression on her face. She knew Hal, having met him once before. "What's going on here?"

"Hal was just leaving." Summer would rather not involve her coworker in her personal problems.

He sent her a dangerous look.

"Okay." Alicia reluctantly retreated.

Summer had the feeling her coworker wouldn't go far. "I wasn't kidding, Hal." She struggled to calm her anxious breathing. "Leave now. I won't risk my job because of you."

"We aren't done with this."

At the sound of footsteps, they both spun to see Quinn appear, his hat still held his hand. He stopped and locked eyes with Hal for a full three seconds before turning to Summer.

"You all right?"

"I'm fine."

"You sure?" Quinn moved toward her, his stance protective.

"Who's this?" Hal demanded.

Summer would have put him off. Unfortunately, Quinn stepped forward before she could insist Hal get out now.

"I'm Quinn Crenshaw. And you are?"

"None of your damn business." Hal's gaze left Quinn only to return, recognition visibly dawning in his eyes. "You the Dempseys' ex-con cousin?"

"Hal!" Summer was aghast. He could be incredibly rude at times.

Quinn didn't flinch or blink or move a single muscle except to talk. "I am Josh and Cole's cousin."

Hal's stare intensified. "They hired you to work at the therapy program."

Dennis, the market manager, must have told Hal. He gleaned a lot of local information, intentionally or unintentionally, by waiting on customers.

"They did," Quinn confirmed.

Hal advanced. "You don't go near my son, you hear me? You do, and I'll call the police."

"Oh, for crying out loud." Summer couldn't believe him. "What's the matter with you?"

"He's a criminal."

"He was found innocent!"

Not only did Alicia return, Martin accompanied her. Being in his early sixties made no difference. He stood up to Hal like a man many years younger.

"Unless you have business with me or this firm, I suggest you vacate the premises immediately. I won't tolerate anyone harassing my employees or my clients."

"If I hear that guy's come within a mile of Teddy, you and I are going to be revisiting our custody agreement." Tossing Quinn one last look, Hal stormed out.

"I'm so, so sorry." Summer's cheeks burned with embarrassment and she held back tears. "I had no idea."

"It's all right," Martin said.

She swore she could hear a silent *Just don't let it happen again* tagged on the end. She didn't blame her boss. Hal's disruption was completely unprofessional. In the morning, at home, she'd call her personal attorney, who'd send a warning to Hal through his attorney.

Why did this have to happen now, in front of Quinn?

"Let me know if you need anything." Quinn touched her shoulder before thanking Martin for his help and leaving.

The gesture itself was subtle yet powerful. It was also kind and delivered when Summer most needed it. She'd remember the feel of Quinn's hand for a long time.

She quickly finished her work for the day and left a few minutes before five in order to reach the mailbox on the first floor before the final pickup.

In the parking lot, she walked to the row where her car was parked—and received her second shock in the last half hour. Quinn's truck was parked in the neighboring spot, and he leaned against the hood, his arms folded over his chest.

SUMMER CAME TO a halt, a mixture of emotions coursing through her. She was glad to see Quinn. She'd also rather have avoided him after the scene with Hal and the threats he'd made.

Was Hal still in the parking lot, watching her from a distance?

"What are you doing here?" she asked Quinn.

"I wanted to make sure you were okay." He pushed off his truck and came toward her, looking heart-stoppingly gorgeous with his confident stride and cowboy hat pulled low.

"I'm fine. Thanks."

She moved her oversize purse from one shoulder to the other in a vain attempt to shield herself from the force of his potent appeal.

"You sure? You look angry, and I'm thinking it's not just at Hal but me, too."

"No, no. What happened isn't your fault. It's entirely his. He shouldn't have said what he did."

"Do you think he's serious? Will he revisit your custody agreement?"

"I don't know what's to revisit. Technically we have joint custody, though he hasn't taken Teddy for more than a couple of hours at a time in, well, years." She had to stop and mentally count how many. "I can't believe he wants full custody, and I can't imagine he'd get it. I'm not an unfit parent."

"You're the furthest thing from an unfit parent there is."

"Thank you." She glanced away, searching for Hal's

car, then back at Quinn. "But just in case Hal is serious and means to make trouble for me…"

"Right. I should go."

Summer instantly felt bad. "Wait. That's not what I meant."

"Don't worry about it." He reached for the door handle on his truck.

"Quinn. Please." She scrubbed her cheek with her free hand. "Hal can be difficult. And he was completely out of line. He had no business coming to my work and no right to insult you."

"He loves his son. I get it."

"He did love Teddy. Once." Summer grimaced. "That wasn't fair. But Hal's feelings for Teddy have changed since the diagnosis. I can't trust him. Not when I believe he's simply trying to look good for the adoption agency. He and his wife recently applied." She groaned. "That wasn't fair, either."

"I won't tell anyone."

She laughed softly. "Maybe you should. I'm not always as nice as people think I am."

"You have a dark side." One corner of Quinn's mouth curved up in the beginnings of a sexy grin. "I'm intrigued."

He wasn't alone.

Summer held in a sigh. He probably had no idea how often kindness and compassion peeked out from behind the rough-around-the-edges demeanor he diligently maintained.

She'd have to watch herself closely if she hoped to guard her heart.

"How'd you get to be so nice?" she asked.

"I'm not nice. Not all the time."

She smiled. "Ah. You're like me. You have a dark side."

"I don't think there was ever a doubt. I did spend the last couple years in prison."

"But you're innocent."

"My temper landed me there. And don't say I was justified," he interrupted when she started to speak. "I could have handled the situation differently and chose not to."

How many people did Summer know who blamed anyone or anything besides themselves for something entirely their fault? It took a lot of courage and strength of character to admit one's mistakes. Yet another reason to like Quinn.

"You didn't answer my question. From what I've heard, prison isn't the kind of place that brings out the best in a person." She discreetly wiped at the perspiration forming on her brow.

Apparently not that discreetly for he said, "It's hot out here. You want to go somewhere with air-conditioning? A coffee shop or a fast food place?"

She appreciated that he didn't offer to take her to happy hour at the closest bar. "I can't. I have to pick up Teddy. His after-school program ends at six sharp. No being late."

"Then you'd better get a move on."

"I will. As soon as you tell me. Why aren't you angry and bitter and resentful and mean? Most people would be in your circumstances."

Removing a pair of sunglasses from his shirt pocket, he slipped them on. She missed being able to stare into his eyes and watch the subtle play of emotions. Quinn said a whole lot without uttering a word.

Funny, he reminded her of Teddy in that regard.

"My father taught me everything I know," Quinn finally said.

"About rodeoing?"

"Yes, and more. He competed for a while and did pretty good. Hundreds of bull rides, maybe thousands, and he never got seriously hurt. Some broken bones, of course, and a few trips to the emergency room. It goes with the territory. But nothing that ever laid him up for long. Ten months after he retired and went to work for a construction company, he was hit by a delivery truck at the job site and thrown fifteen feet onto solid concrete. I was seven at the time, but I remember everything. The weeks in the hospital. The months of physical therapy. Endless trips to the doctor. He was never the same afterward, and neither were we."

"I'm so sorry." Summer wondered if he'd put on his sunglasses to hide his pain.

"Traumatic brain injury. It's a term that covers a lot. People assumed he was crippled from the accident. Actually, the part of his brain controlling movement was affected. It sends the wrong signals to his limbs. Twenty-six years later and he still can't read for more than a few minutes before the words become a jumble. About once a month he'll disappear into his room for two days with a migraine no amount of medication can alleviate."

"Wow. That must be hard. For him and your whole family." Another reason for his acceptance of Teddy.

"My father's the same good, gentle person he always was. Funny. Easygoing. He'd give anyone the shirt off his back. Even strangers."

"He sounds like a wonderful man."

"People aren't always nice, kids especially, and they teased him unmercifully. I suppose it's to be expected. What I can't understand and never will is why adults tease him, too. The same people he'd lend the shirt off his back mimic his limp or halting speech when he's not looking. Sometimes they do it when he's looking, then slap him on the back or jab him in the ribs as if that makes it okay."

"Bullies come in all ages." Summer was well aware of

that sad fact. And Teddy wasn't always the target. She received her share of cruel comments and dirty looks.

"I grew up tough and with a bad temper that took very little to trigger," Quinn said.

"It would be hard not to develop a temper after what you've been through."

"Prison wasn't the first time I spent behind bars. I've been in jail more than once, and not for unpaid traffic tickets."

If he intended to shock Summer, he hadn't. "For minor infractions, I'm sure."

"Fighting isn't minor. Neither is drunk and disorderly."

He didn't have to add that a previous record hadn't served him well at his trial.

"I haven't had a drink since my arrest. Personal choice. I've been given a second chance, and I don't intend to blow it. I may not get another one."

"A good philosophy to have. I couldn't agree with you more."

"My parents had every right to be angry with me and disappointed and ashamed. Only they weren't. My father told me once during a visit that what mattered most was the kind of man I became, not the man I was. I remember those words every day."

"He's a wise man, and you're wise to have heeded him."

Quinn shrugged. "You're never too old to learn, I guess. Or, in my case, too stubborn."

Summer's phone beeped, her reminder that she had thirty minutes to pick up Teddy. Setting an automatic daily alarm helped keep her on track when she got busy.

She swiped her phone screen, silencing the alarm. "I have to go." The learning center was a twenty-minute drive. She had just enough time to make it, barring any traffic jams. "Will I see you later at the riding arena?"

Convinced he was about to say no, he surprised her by nodding. "You will."

She stifled the impulse to hug him.

Parting, Quinn got into his truck and Summer her car. He waited while she backed out of her parking space. She gave him a little wave before pulling ahead.

Timing was everything. Why couldn't she have met Quinn three years ago, before the assault outside the bar? Four years ago, before he'd met Jenny and when Summer was newly divorced from Hal?

She immediately dismissed the notion. If they'd met then, Quinn wouldn't have had his daughter and, to be honest, Summer wouldn't have been ready for a relationship so soon after the end of her marriage.

What about the future? In a year, maybe two, she and Quinn might be in entirely different places. Perhaps then they'd be able and ready to act on their mutual attraction.

Crazy thoughts. She had to put an end to them.

Navigating traffic, she tried to get to the learning center as quickly as possible while not breaking any speeding laws. The center charged an outrageous fee for every minute a parent arrived late to pick up his or her child. That wasn't, however, the real reason she hurried. Teddy became very agitated when she was late. Summer wasn't in the frame of mind to cope with one of his outbursts, especially after the confrontation with Hal.

She reached the center with five minutes to spare. Opening the door to the activity room where the after-school program took place, she was met by an empty room and a surprised staff member.

"Mrs. Goodwyn." The young woman appeared confused. "I wasn't expecting you."

"Hi, Heidi." Strange thing to say. Summer glanced around. "Where's Teddy? The restroom?"

"He's gone."

A spear of alarm sliced through her. "Gone! Where?"

"His father picked him up. Thirty minutes ago."

Hal? No, impossible. Summer's knees went weak. "You let him take Teddy?"

"He's on the list. And he showed me his driver's license."

Hal *never* picked up Teddy. Why today?

"Is there a problem?" the staff member asked in a worried voice.

Summer didn't answer. She was already out the door, cell phone in hand, speed dialing Hal's number.

Chapter Four

Summer wasn't there. She'd told Quinn she'd see him that evening at the ranch, but there was no sign of her or Teddy.

He'd used Chubbs's vision loss, and the need to monitor the old gelding to make sure he remained reliable, as an excuse to hang around the arena. That and helping Cara saddle the horses—he'd promised Josh he wouldn't let her lift anything heavy.

Now, twenty minutes into the lesson, five children walked their horses in a placid circle under the direction of the head instructor. The children laughed, smiled and shouted excitedly while their parents beamed at each other and called out encouragements.

Quinn glanced over his shoulder at the parking area, his agitation increasing. Where was Summer? Maybe he should give her a call on the chance something had happened. Her ex-husband, no prize in Quinn's opinion, had left the law office angry and, also in Quinn's opinion, gunning for bear. He'd watched the man exit the building, jog across the parking lot toward his vehicle and then burn rubber as he pulled onto the street. Quinn was certain the man had a specific destination in mind and hoped it wasn't Summer's place.

His fingers itched to remove his phone from his pocket and dial her number. He resisted, forcing himself to stand at the arena railing, observing Chubbs. The old gelding diligently followed Pancake while carefully transporting his young rider, a girl about Teddy's age. Only once did he swing his head around to give George Clooney behind him a warning stare.

Quinn shifted, scratched his jaw and readjusted his hat. Would Cara know where Summer was? They were best friends. How obvious would he be if he asked?

"There you are."

He turned to find Cara heading his way. "What's going on?"

"You expecting company? You look anxious."

"Just watching the class."

She moved closer and studied the riders. Each one was assisted by a staff member who walked along beside them.

"How's Chubbs doing?"

"Great," he said. "As long as no other horse gets closer than five feet behind him."

They chatted for a few minutes and then Quinn spotted Summer's familiar red car from the corner of his eye.

"Finally, she made it." Cara spoke more to herself than Quinn.

He couldn't tell from her tone if she'd known Summer was going to be late or not. Seeing the driver's side door open, spotting the tight expression on Summer's face even from this distance, he had to stop himself from rushing over.

No reason he couldn't meander. "I'll get Stargazer ready for Teddy."

Quinn felt the heat from Cara's gaze on him as he headed to Summer's car and not the stalls where Stargazer waited. He didn't care. He had to find out if she was okay. When he got there, she was standing at the open rear door, waiting for Teddy to climb out of his booster seat.

"Come on, sweetheart. Don't you want to see Stargazer? She loves it when you brush and pet her."

The boy rocked back and forth in his seat and hummed.

"How's it going?" Quinn asked.

"Hey." She exhaled wearily. "Okay."

"Can I help?"

She shook her head. "I'm not sure there's anything you could do."

"I'll bring Stargazer around. That might encourage him."

"Would you?" Her smile radiated joy and appreciation. "Thank you so much."

Quinn felt his heart lift, as if the heavy weight he'd been carrying these past three years had suddenly shrunk by half.

"Be right back."

He hurried to the stalls and fetched Stargazer. With her small size and sweet nature, the mare was a perfect match for Teddy. Slipping on her halter, Quinn led her to the tack room where he grabbed a brush and hoof pick, then returned with Stargazer to Summer's car. Teddy hadn't moved from his seat.

"Sweetheart, look who's here."

Summer stepped away, allowing Quinn to bring Stargazer right up to the open door. The curious mare extended her head just inside the car, her nostrils flaring as she sniffed the air.

Teddy stopped rocking and humming. His left hand jerked reflexively, and he made a garbled sound.

"That's right," Summer said happily. "It's Stargazer."

Quinn hadn't gotten the horse's name from the sound Teddy made. No matter. Summer was happy and, it seemed, Teddy was, as well. Angling his head, he reached his arm out to pet Stargazer's nose.

"Haws, haws."

"Yes." Summer breathed a sigh of relief. "Horse."

Teddy threw off his unbuckled seat belt and climbed out of the booster seat. Scrambling from the car with an agility that impressed Quinn, he hugged Stargazer's neck and rubbed his cheek along her soft hide.

"How about that?" Quinn chuckled. "The horse is a miracle worker."

"She is." Summer stared longingly at her son, who murmured unintelligible words into Stargazer's neck.

Was she wishing she could hold her son as he held the mare or simply glad that whatever terrible thing had been tormenting him had finally let go, if only temporarily?

"What do you say, buddy?" Quinn held out the brush to Teddy. "You ready to give her a good grooming?"

Teddy released Stargazer and met Quinn's gaze for a brief second before taking the brush. Quinn walked the mare to the rear of Summer's car where there was more room to maneuver. Teddy approached Stargazer and began methodically running the brush along her side and down her legs. The mare snorted lustily and lowered her head, appearing to relish the attention.

Quinn thought about leaving, but then Summer spoke, giving him reason to believe she'd read his earlier thoughts.

"I'm always amazed at how he interacts with the horses. Our dog, Paw Paw, too. Why is it special-needs children can form bonds with animals when they don't or can't with people? I see it all the time with the students at the learning center."

"Speaking for myself, I've rarely met a horse or dog I didn't like. Now, people on the other hand…"

She laughed softly, then quickly became quiet. "Hal picked up Teddy from after-school care without telling me. It's why we're late tonight and why Teddy's upset. He doesn't adapt well to changes in his routine. When I arrived at Hal's, Teddy was in the throes of a major meltdown. Hal and his wife acted like they had everything under control. They didn't, and I'm sure they were secretly thrilled I showed up when I did."

Quinn didn't like learning that his suspicions regarding Hal were founded. "Can he do that? Just take Teddy from school?"

"As was pointed out to me by the girl on duty, he's on the list. Of course, I have his name added in case of an emergency. But he's never picked up Teddy. Not once in the year he's been going to the center."

"Why today?"

"A power struggle, I suppose."

"It's my fault. I'm sorry."

She shook her head. "I don't buy that for one minute. Hal's problems are with me."

Quinn wasn't convinced. The fact that Hal had picked up Teddy from school literally minutes after he and Quinn met was too much of a coincidence. Whatever Quinn and Summer had, friendship or something more, was bound to cause her trouble. Better he maintain his distance.

"I should get back to the lessons." He hitched his chin in the direction of the arena. "Cara's waiting."

"Okay." She gave him a little smile. "See you later."

"Staaa."

Quinn looked down to see Teddy had a hold of his belt, the same one with the galloping horses.

"Staaa," the boy repeated.

"Mr. Crenshaw has things he needs to do," Summer said with forced cheerfulness.

Teddy grunted, a severe frown creasing his brow.

Against his better judgment, Quinn relented. "Just a few more minutes."

Teddy's frown promptly vanished, and he resumed brushing Stargazer.

"But only if you clean her hooves." Quinn passed the lead rope to Summer and removed the hoof pick from his pocket. Bending down beside Stargazer, he lifted her front leg and balanced the upturned hoof above his knee. "Well?" he said to Teddy when Teddy didn't move.

Slowly, very slowly, the boy came and stood across from Quinn, the mare's hoof between them. Quinn showed Teddy how to clean the hoof, digging out and knocking free clumps of dirt and tiny stones from the shallow grooves. Teddy stared, fixated.

"You try." He handed the pick to Teddy, observing him carefully.

The boy managed to free the last of the dirt from beneath the metal shoe.

"Good. Now we do the others." Together, they repeated the process on all three remaining hooves. "Can you walk her?"

Quinn indicated to Summer that she should relinquish the mare to Teddy. He clutched the lead rope to his middle and started forward, Stargazer plodding along behind him.

"Don't go far," Summer said. "Stay where I can see you."

"What's the reason he hasn't ridden yet?" Quinn asked. "He seems comfortable around horses."

"It's not that. He won't let anyone lift him into the saddle."

"What about a stepladder? He could climb onto Stargazer himself."

"We tried that during his first lesson. He'd have none of it."

"Might be worth another try."

She searched his face, seeking what, he wasn't sure.

"You're an interesting man, Quinn Crenshaw. Not what I expected. Not in the least."

"What *were* you expecting?"

"Someone angry and surly and brutish."

"Brutish?" He was reminded of Popeye's nemesis Brutus. "Should I be insulted?"

"You're a good person."

"I've been on my best behavior since coming here. In truth, every day's a struggle."

"Trust me, I understand."

He supposed she did, more than most people.

Knowing it was wrong, he leaned in and lowered his head, the temptation to inhale her subtle fragrance and hear the slight intake of her breath too hard to resist.

"Quinn." His name was a whisper on her lips. "I wish things were different."

"I do, too."

Kissing her would be a simple matter of capturing her mouth with his. He didn't, though his gut told him she'd respond with an ardor she kept hidden.

"I…um…" She hesitated.

"Right." Hadn't he vowed mere minutes ago to avoid causing her trouble?

Quinn retreated a step, then walked away. Mistakes were easy to make, and he'd committed too many already in his life.

Eyes on the prize, he told himself. For Summer, it was her son's health, happiness and quality of life. For Quinn, finding his daughter. No kiss, even with someone as appealing as Summer, was worth the risk.

"I CAN BARELY BREATHE." Cole Dempsey yanked at his collar, loosening the black leather and silver bolo tie, then unfastening the tiny top buttons on his white dress shirt.

Quinn sympathized. His collar also fit like a choke hold. He thought he could tolerate it for the few hours he'd be required to wear the tuxedo. Josh and Cara's wedding was in two weeks. They'd picked the Valley Community Church for their small, private ceremony, followed by a celebration of marriage at Dos Estrellas with over two hundred friends and family scheduled to attend.

Cole, as best man, would be sharing groomsman duties along with Quinn and Gabe, whose wedding to Reese was finally decided on and taking place next spring.

"Let me check it." The clerk flipped Cole's collar partially inside out in order to read the label. "We may need to go up a neck size."

"May?" Cole asked, pretending to gasp for air.

"If you wait one minute, I'll be right back with another shirt for you to try on."

Cole nodded, then grunted when the tall, slim and impeccably dressed man speed walked away from them. He unfastened another button.

"Only for my brother would I wear this monkey suit."

Quinn observed himself in the mirrors. Multiple images from various angles moved in unison as he turned to the left, then right. The tux—black, Western cut and an identical version of the one Cole wore—was a lot fancier than anything he'd worn before, including to his high school prom. It also beat the heck out of a prison jumpsuit.

He tugged on the jacket sleeves. "I've worn worse."

If his cousin understood Quinn's reference, he gave no indication. "You're going to need to buy a new hat. That one's ready for the trash heap."

Quinn grabbed the crown and shoved the hat lower onto his head. Cole was right. He'd have to find the money for a new Stetson. This one, not new when he'd been arrested, showed its age.

Most of his first paycheck from the horse therapy program had gone to the private investigator he'd rehired. Even then, it was only enough to cover one day's service.

He'd get another paycheck next week. Still plenty of time to buy a new hat before the wedding.

"I thought when we were done here, you'd come with me to the sanctuary." Cole stood at the set of mirrors next to Quinn's, contemplating his reflection.

"Sure. What's going on?"

"The next mustang adoption event is in three months. We need to handpick potential horses and begin training them, figuring out which ones are adoptable and which ones aren't. The event raises a lot of money for the sanctuary and generates income for the ranch, too. Without the mustang sanctuary, Dos Estrellas would still be operating in the red."

Quinn had heard about the ranch's past financial woes from Josh. "Okay. Sounds good."

Cole gave himself a long look in the mirrors.

Quinn suppressed a grin. Cole might have complained about wearing the tuxedo, but he clearly liked what he saw. And with good reason. The tuxes brought out the best in both of them.

What would Summer think when she got a look at him? She, of course, was Cara's maid of honor. Cole's girlfriend, Violet, had been paired with Quinn while Gabe and his fiancée, Reese, were the third couple. At least, Quinn thought that was right. He admitted to some confusion. The intricacies of the Dempsey family weren't always easy to understand.

The clerk returned with a new shirt for Cole to try on. He took it and disappeared into the dressing room, leaving the clerk to fuss over Quinn. The man checked and marked the length of Quinn's pant legs and jacket sleeves for the third time. Just when Quinn was growing impatient, Cole returned. The clerk immediately and thankfully abandoned Quinn. A few minutes later, Cole deemed the shirt to be a better fit. Finishing up, they changed back into their regular clothes.

"You hungry? Let's stop for some lunch," Cole said without waiting for Quinn's response. They'd driven to Scottsdale in his truck, which, Quinn supposed, put him in charge. Not that he'd argue. His stomach had been growling for the past twenty minutes.

They decided on a Mexican restaurant, a hole in the wall as Quinn's father called them. The kind of hole-in-the-wall restaurant with great food, he decided the moment they walked inside and were assaulted by an array of tantalizing aromas.

"You getting settled in okay?" Cole asked over chips and salsa while they waited for their food.

"Fine."

"How's the apartment? I know it's kind of small."

"You've got to be kidding. Compared to where I've been living of late, it's a mansion. I turn a corner and get lost."

Cole sat back in his chair, a twinkle in his eyes. "Glad to see you didn't lose your sense of humor."

"I did. For a while."

"Then I'm glad to see it's back." He leaned forward and, snaring a chip, dunked it in the salsa. "You're the third one of us to live in that apartment. Josh moved in after gaining custody of Nathan and Kimberly, and I lived there a couple of months until Vi agreed to marry me."

"You two getting hitched?" This was the first Quinn had heard of it. "When?"

Cole helped himself to more chips and salsa. "Don't say anything. We're eloping this weekend to Sedona. Already have the chapel booked and dinner reservations at the Red Rock Steak House. Josh and Cara are coming for the day to be our witnesses. Vi and I are staying through till Monday."

"I'm happy for you, cousin."

"Thanks for not saying it's about time."

"Well…"

Violet was almost seven months pregnant. Quinn had figured the two of them would get married before the baby was born, so the announcement didn't come as a surprise.

"We don't want to steal Josh and Cara's thunder," Cole said. "They've been planning their wedding for months. But we couldn't wait much longer. I wouldn't wait. I want to be married when our daughter is born."

Now, *this* was a surprise. "You're having a girl? Congratulations."

Cole grimaced. "Damn, I let another secret slip out. Vi's gonna have my hide. You have to give me your word you won't say anything."

"I promise."

"I'd invite you to the wedding, but we need someone besides Gabe to cover for us at the ranch while we're gone. That, and the rest of the family's bound to notice we're gone. Maybe you can help throw them off track. At least until Josh and Cara get home."

"I'll do my best."

"How's the search for your daughter coming?"

The abrupt change in subject took Quinn momentarily aback. "Nothing new. Summer's boss is helping me. He had some good advice to offer and some leads. He's also going to see if he can speed up the process of clearing my record."

"What record? You're innocent."

"Not that easy. There's a lengthy process. Until then, my record follows me. Probably for years. Maybe forever.

If anyone runs a background check on me, my felony conviction will pop up and not my exoneration."

"Jeez, man. That sucks."

"Yeah. Tell me about it. One of the many injustices of our so-called justice system." Quinn wasn't as accepting of his circumstances as he tried to make people believe. "He also suggested suing the state for compensation."

"You can do that?"

Quinn nodded. "He thinks I have a chance of getting a decent settlement. And, frankly, I could use the money."

Their lunch came, and they dug in. Quinn decided he'd eaten better steak chimichangas. Once. Years ago. The food here was that fantastic.

"How do you feel about learning you're a dad?"

Cole was the first person to ask that question. Most people wanted to know if Quinn resented Jenny for lying and keeping his daughter a secret from him. Perhaps Cole's curiosity stemmed from his own impending fatherhood and the many changes about to occur.

"I'm still getting used to the idea. Though, to be honest, she's not part of my life yet. I don't really feel like a dad."

"I get that. Same goes for me." Cole talked around a large bite of chile rellenos. "The waiting is tough."

Except Cole's wait had an end in sight, and it would happen in the delivery room. The search for Quinn's daughter could last for months, possibly years.

"Much as I'd like to find her," Quinn said, "part of me hopes it's not before Summer's boss can get my record cleared." *If* he could. Quinn hated the idea of his daughter having a felon for a father.

"Here's to a speedy process." Cole raised his iced tea glass and clinked it with Quinn's. "Speaking of Summer, I hear you two have been hanging out."

"I wouldn't say hanging out." Had someone noticed

them standing a little too close at her car the other day, a hairbreadth away from kissing, and made a comment? Or sitting together in the courtyard at his welcome party? "Her son's in the therapy program. I work with the therapy horses."

"She's a good person."

"I'm not going to corrupt her," Quinn bit out, letting a flash of temper show.

"Hey." Cole held up a hand. "I'm not criticizing. Simply making conversation."

His cousin's response came quickly and smoothly enough to be true. Quinn, however, couldn't shake his doubts. Intended or not, the remark had sounded like a warning, the same one he'd given himself over and over since meeting Summer.

They finished their lunch, their talk centering mostly on ranching matters. When Quinn tried to buy lunch, Cole insisted on picking up the tab. He let Cole pay only when his cousin agreed that Quinn would buy the next time.

Violet phoned Cole shortly after they were on the road. Quinn couldn't help listening to their conversation, Cole sat a mere three feet away. They didn't discuss anything of importance, which made it all the nicer to hear. Jenny was the last person Quinn had called for no reason other than to say hi, and that had been before his arrest.

Summer came to mind, but he quickly dismissed thoughts of her. She wasn't anyone he could or should consider calling on a whim.

With the sweltering midday heat bearing down on them, they decided to drive rather than ride to the mustang sanctuary and took Cole's truck instead. Behind the ranch, beyond the first rocky slope where fenced horse pastures gave way to open cattle grazing lands, the dirt road narrowed to a rough trail.

Quinn had to hold on to his hat more than once as the truck bounced and rocked. Cole was a notoriously fast driver. At each gate, he got out, waited until Cole drove through and closed the gate behind him.

The roughly twelve hundred head of cattle on the ranch were divided into several smaller groups and regularly moved from section to section. Yearlings, the ones headed to the fall sale, were currently pastured in sections one and two. In this heat, and with the late summer monsoon season yet to start, grass had started becoming scarce. In order to keep the herd of yearlings and the pregnant cows well fed, Cole and his brothers were supplementing the regular feed with hay. Two semi-truck loads had been scheduled for delivery later in the week.

Another half mile west, they reached the gate connecting the mustang sanctuary to the cattle grazing lands. Cole and Josh's late father August had granted Cara exclusive use of the sanctuary in his will for as long as she chose or as long as the Dempseys resided on the ranch. With her marrying into the family, the sanctuary appeared to have a bright and secure future.

"Look at that." Cole pointed to their right. "We've got company."

Quinn watched through the window as a group of about fifty mustangs galloped over the rise toward them. At the front of the herd was a sleek buckskin mare. Head raised, neck arched and hooves flying, she charged the truck.

No, not charged. Just when the group neared, she turned and ran alongside the truck, matching its speed mile for mile.

The sight was an inspiring one, and it filled Quinn with a sense of both wonder and contentment. Coming to Mustang Valley had been the right decision. How long he'd stay depended on if—no, when—he found Jenny and his daughter.

"That buckskin's got some spirit," Quinn said a short time later. "She'll make someone a good horse."

"Yeah, if you can catch her."

"I can." He glanced at Cole and grinned.

They'd parked the truck just inside the sanctuary and were standing with their arms resting on the hood. The herd had followed them the entire distance and now grazed peacefully on the nearby rise as if they hadn't just been galloping for five straight minutes.

"This I got to see." Cole went over to the passenger door, opened it, reached behind the seat and retrieved a coiled lariat.

Quinn eyed his cousin. "You're kidding."

"Time to put your money where your mouth is."

"All right."

Quinn went around to the truck bed and rummaged through the various piles for a pair of leather gloves. Donning them, he took the lariat from Cole and ran it through his hands while slowly approaching the herd.

Like the hammer the other day, the rope felt good resting against his palm. He'd picked one up only a few times since his release, throwing some practice tosses behind his grandparents' barn.

"I'm more used to roping calves," he said over his shoulder.

"Chickening out?"

"No way."

The buckskin's head popped up as he approached, along with several other mustangs'. She watched with growing unease but stood her ground. Quinn liked her even more.

"That's a good girl," he cooed.

She really was a beauty, and he considered her strong

personality and feisty temperament to be desirable qualities. When he caught her, and he would, she'd be a hard horse to give up.

Raising his arm, he began swinging the rope over his head.

"Easy does it," he murmured as he took aim.

The buckskin flinched but stayed rooted in place as if daring him.

Just then, Quinn's cell phone rang from his shirt pocket and he froze, his concentration broken. The ring tone was the one he'd assigned to the private investigator.

Lowering the rope, he reached into his pocket. Swiping the screen was hard with his gloves on. Hurriedly, he ripped them off and barked, "Hello," afraid he'd been too late and missed the call.

"Quinn, it's Rodney. I have news. Good news."

Quinn dropped the lariat and his gloves onto the ground, spooking the buckskin. When she ran off, Quinn barely noticed.

Chapter Five

"Haws, haws, haws." Teddy rocked back and forth in his booster seat, chanting incessantly.

"We'll be there soon, sweetie," Summer assured him from the driver's seat.

They were heading to the ranch. Tonight was Teddy's therapy session, hence his excitement. To the casual observer, it might be difficult to distinguish the difference between when he was happy and when he was upset. Summer, of course, could always tell.

"It won't be long now." She checked the rearview mirror, satisfied he was fine. "Another few minutes."

The scenic drive from her house on the other side of Mustang Valley to Dos Estrellas always lifted her spirits. Must be all the good memories associated with the ranch. Besides Teddy's therapy sessions and her best friend Cara working there, Summer now had Quinn's presence to eagerly anticipate.

"Man, man," Teddy called out, kicking the back of her seat with his sneakers.

She ignored the thumping. "Yes, Quinn will be there."

At least, he usually was. She hoped he'd be there. For Teddy's sake. He'd grown quite fond of Quinn and responded well to him.

Fine, she admitted. For her sake, too. She hadn't been

alone with Quinn for days. Not since their near kiss. Unless it wasn't a near kiss and entirely a figment of her imagination. After his abrupt departure, she'd been unsure.

If she concentrated, she could recall the thrill that had wound through her at his nearness and the delicious shiver his touch had evoked. Granted, she hadn't been with a man for years and might just be hungry for intimacy with someone she found attractive. Did three awkward dates in four years, set up by well-intentioned friends and ending with promises to call that never materialized, count?

Unlike with those other men, she'd been at ease with Quinn from the start. Perhaps because he'd met Teddy first and understood her situation without her having to explain a whole lot. Perhaps, and more likely, because there wasn't anything between them other than friendship.

Who was she kidding? For her part, at least, there was an intense and sizzling attraction. She firmly believed it was mutual. She also believed it unwise for them to act on it.

Too bad. Summer allowed herself to expel a long, sad sigh. Too, too bad.

"Here we are," she said cheerily, pulling into the long drive leading to the ranch.

Passing the Dempsey house, she continued on to the horse stables and parking area. There were always a lot of cars, what with one helper per child during the lessons. As yet, all they needed from Teddy's helper was assistance getting Stargazer from her stall. He still refused to be lifted onto the saddle. Perhaps tonight Quinn might help her with a stepladder.

Once she and Teddy were out of the car and walking toward the arena, she automatically glanced about for Quinn. She didn't see him right away but thought nothing of it. He was always there during the therapy program lessons.

Her certainty waned as the minutes passed without his making an appearance.

"Man, man," Teddy said, running ahead of Summer.

She hurried after him. "Wait up, sweetie. Quinn's not here."

Had he gotten more news about his daughter and left the ranch? Summer had worked from home the last couple of days and knew only a minimal amount of information. She wasn't sure if Quinn's daughter had actually been located or if there was just a potential lead. Alicia might have told Summer the details if she called the office, but she refused to appear nosy. Her coworker had already accused Summer of being smitten.

With the assistance of their assigned staff member, Teddy groomed Stargazer, brushing the horse's coat until it gleamed. When he became suddenly agitated, they decided to walk with Stargazer around the grounds. Teddy hummed as the horse dutifully followed him, occasionally sniffing his hair or shirt.

Summer tried not to be jealous. If she placed a hand on Teddy, he'd shriek or flinch or swat her away.

They were on the second circuit when Summer noticed two things. The tune Teddy hummed less resembled the five notes he always repeated and almost sounded like the melody to the Eensie Weensie Spider—this was a big step. A moment later, she spotted Quinn in the round pen working with a horse. She attempted to tamp down the sudden gladness rising in her, but her wildly beating heart would have none of it.

Teddy spotted Quinn, too, and calling "Man, man," he broke into a run.

Summer wasn't sure what to do until the staff member volunteered to take Stargazer. For the second time, she hurried toward Quinn. What choice did she have? It wasn't as if she purposely sought him out.

Teddy stopped at the round pen and lowered his head to peer through the rail at Quinn. He made a sound Summer hadn't heard before. She thought it might be Quinn's name.

Hearing Teddy, he turned. "Hey, buddy." His gaze landed on Summer. "Hi to you, too," he said when she reached Teddy's side.

"Are we bothering you?" she asked. Her smile felt ridiculously wide. His answering one lit yet another spark inside her, as if she needed more sparks.

"Not at all." He stood in the center of the round pen, a long line attached to the buckskin's halter. "We're having our first official training session."

"How's it going?"

"Well…" He tipped his cowboy hat back off his face and wiped his brow with his shirt sleeve. "She's a little greener than I first figured and a lot more stubborn than I counted on."

"She is pretty."

The corners of his mouth turned up. "She is that."

Summer worried that she might be showing her ignorance. Until she met Cara a few years ago at the local church where they were both attending support groups—Cara's for grief after the death of her young son, Summer's for families of special-needs children—she'd had little experience with horses.

"I'm assuming she's one of the mustangs."

"Cole and I are getting thirty or forty of them ready for the next adoption event."

That was months away, but perhaps it was never too early to start. Cara had been in charge of the administrative duties at the last adoption event, which raised considerable money for the sanctuary. Teddy and Josh had also put on a display with one of the rehabilitated mustangs that had been a rousing success.

Naturally, Summer had volunteered to help out again. It appeared she might be working with Quinn on this one. With the upcoming wedding and related activities, they'd be seeing a lot of each other. Not that she cared.

"I'm sure she'll find a good home." Again, she didn't know a lot. This horse, however, seemed to have a lot going for it. Big, strong and clearly spirited.

"Maybe." Quinn clucked and waved his free arm to get the horse moving.

"You don't think you can train her?"

"Oh, I can train her." Appreciation shone on his face and colored his voice. "I just may decide to buy her for myself."

It was easy to see Quinn riding the buckskin. They were a well-suited pair.

Beside her, Teddy watched, completely content and quiet as a mouse. Summer relaxed, the tension seeping slowly out of her. These were rare moments. Once a day, maybe twice if she was lucky, she could enjoy herself without any guilt or worry.

"Whoa," Quinn said in a booming voice, commanding the buckskin to stop trotting. When she did, he approached cautiously and held out his hand. "Good girl." Reaching her, he patted her neck and unsnapped the long line attached to her halter. Winding it into a coil, he hung the line on a corral post.

Free, the horse meandered off to a corner of the pen and, resting her head on the railing, stared at the horses in the arena. A mild breeze tossed her fetlock and mane.

Summer joined Quinn at the railing. It was high, reaching her shoulders. Quinn was several inches taller than she.

She liked looking up at him. Despite her independence, despite her pro stance on feminism, Quinn's height and powerful bearing made her feel protected and attractive and, yes, sexy. What would her mother, a staunch women's activist from the seventies, say? What would she say about Quinn?

"The private investigator found my daughter."

"Is he sure?" Summer knew from working at the law firm all these years that leads could appear promising in the beginning only to prove wrong or turn cold in the end.

"He's sure. She and Jenny are living in a small Oregon town called Seaside. Jenny hasn't married and didn't change her last name or assume a new identity. I don't think she saw the need. She probably assumed I'd be in prison for years, that her friend didn't tell about our daughter and I'd have no reason to track her down."

"Does she know she's been located?"

"Marty's hired a local attorney to make contact with her. That's supposed to happen today or tomorrow. There are steps, so I'm told."

Summer knew most of them. For starters, Jenny needed to be advised that Quinn had not only been released, he was exonerated and wanted to make contact with his daughter. Learning that, she might willingly grant Quinn visitation and perhaps even shared custody. Naturally, paternity would have to be established and a DNA test performed.

"I'm really glad for you," she said, and she meant it.

"Me, too." His expression was a combination of excitement and shyness. "I have pictures."

"Really?" Summer smiled.

Quinn was already reaching for his phone. He swiped and tapped the screen several times. A moment later, he handed the phone to her through the railing.

"It's not a great picture," Quinn said. "The PI took it from a distance."

Even so, Summer could make out enough of the little

girl's features to see she resembled Quinn. Dark wavy hair, dark eyes and a much too serious expression. She played in what appeared to be a backyard sandbox.

"She's adorable."

"There's more." Quinn pointed to the phone, indicating Summer should scroll to another picture.

She went through the six photos, each one cuter than the last. Jenny was in most of them, and Summer couldn't help studying the woman who had loved Quinn only to abandon him and take their child far away.

She wanted to hate Jenny, but what she saw in the pictures was a mother who adored her child and would go to any length to protect her from what she perceived as a threat. Summer would do the same for Teddy, except, in her opinion, Quinn was no threat.

She returned his phone. "Did you learn her name?"

"Corrine."

"I like it."

"That was Jenny's grandmother's name." He grew quiet. "Corrine'll be three on October tenth."

Being a parent for almost three years and having no idea—Summer couldn't fathom it. Neither could she fathom what Quinn must be going through. His entire life had been turned upside down, not once but multiple times since that fateful night in the bar.

Her gaze went to Teddy, who stood at the railing staring at the buckskin. She hadn't been apart from her son more than a day since his birth. It was a struggle at times, especially when his behavior was at its worse, but also very rewarding.

"When will you hear from the local attorney?" she asked.

Rather than answer, Quinn walked to the gate, exited the corral and met up with her at the railing. She noted a spring to his step she hadn't seen before and guessed it was the result of hearing his daughter had been located.

Maybe a little of that spring was from nearing her. She shouldn't wish that to be the case but did anyway.

"Marty's supposed to call me as soon as he hears."

"How do you think Jenny's going to react, learning you've been released and exonerated?"

"I'm not sure. I hope she'll do right by me and let me visit Corrine."

Summer hoped so, too, and could tell from the longing in Quinn's voice he hoped for more. Unfortunately, she had reservations. Jenny hadn't done right by Quinn so far and, unlike his family, hadn't believed him when he swore he was innocent. And this was someone who supposedly loved him.

"Let me know if there's anything I can do to help," Summer said.

Quinn startled her by touching her cheek. "You've done a lot for me already. I can't begin to thank you."

She didn't reply. She couldn't, not when the intensity of his gaze and tenderness of his caress drew her in completely.

Without thinking, without giving herself a chance to reconsider, she threw her arms around his neck and hugged him. Her body instinctively molded to his, and her head rested on his shoulder. For a moment, he froze. She feared he wouldn't respond, would leave her hanging there. Or, more correctly, hanging on to him.

Then magic happened, and he circled her waist with his arms. They were strong and powerful and anchored her to him with a surety and confidence she found incredibly sexy.

Closing her eyes, she inhaled deeply. Wouldn't it be

wonderful if they could hug indefinitely? At least for a few more exquisite minutes?

"Maw, Maw, Maw."

Teddy! Oh, my God. She quickly released Quinn and stepped away, shock rendering her speechless. How could she have forgotten they weren't alone? It was so unlike her.

SUMMER WAS VERY PRETTY. Prettier still when she was embarrassed and tripping over her words. Quinn found it impossible not to smile.

The hug they'd shared was innocent. Mostly. There'd been nothing inappropriate for Teddy to see. Yet Summer acted as if she and Quinn had been caught in a compromising situation.

"Y-yes, sweetie," she said. "I, uh, see. It's very…interesting."

Teddy was staring at a beetle crawling along the corral railing. He probably hadn't even seen Summer and Quinn hugging.

"We should…go." Summer might have been speaking to Teddy or to Quinn, it wasn't clear. Then again, she could have been speaking to herself.

He didn't want her to leave. Other than Marty, she was the only one who knew Corrine had been located. They had shared more than a hug.

"Wait," he said. "I have an idea," he continued before Summer could voice an objection. "How about we fetch Stargazer, put a saddle on her and see if Teddy's willing to ride?"

Her eyes narrowed with uncertainty. "Don't you have somewhere to be or something you need to do?"

"Nothing that can't wait."

"What about the horse?"

Quinn regarded the buckskin. "I'll put her away later.

She's fine in the corral for now." He motioned to Teddy. "Let's go, son, and bring Stargazer. We're going riding."

Summer shook her head. "He won't come with you. Not the first time. I usually have to coax him—"

Teddy made a liar of his mother and started toward Quinn. Walking alongside him, he hooked a finger through Quinn's belt loop and began humming. Afraid the boy would let go, Quinn said nothing.

Summer walked along his other side, talking nervously and glancing frequently at Teddy. She must have noticed him holding on to Quinn's belt loop. What did she think? Was she hurt that Teddy responded to Quinn or happy her son had made a connection with someone? It was hard to tell.

Finding the staff member and retrieving Stargazer, they tethered the horse to the hitching post outside the tack room. After assuring the woman they'd be fine, she left to attend to another student. Quinn chose a youth saddle from the array in the tack room and a bridle with a gentle bit, although Teddy probably wouldn't actually guide the horse. The reins were for him to hold on to and to give him a sense of security.

"Do you really think he'll get on the horse?" Summer gave him a skeptical look.

"I do."

"Hmm." She stood off to the side, fidgeting.

Teddy hadn't moved from Stargazer's head and continued to stroke her nose. Unlike his mother, he appeared calm and collected.

"He's been around horses enough to know what a saddle and bridle are used for." Quinn adjusted the girth. "If he were scared or unwilling, he'd have let us know by now. We'd probably be chasing him around the ranch."

"Wait until he sees the stepladder," Summer said.

A moment later, Quinn retrieved it from the tack room. He also brought one of the therapy program's harnesses. While confident Teddy would climb up onto Stargazer, Quinn was less convinced he'd tolerate the harness being attached. That would necessitate a lot of touching and, once on, it might feel restricting.

He'd have to try. There was no way he'd take Teddy riding without safety precautions.

"You ready, son?"

Quinn positioned the stepladder next to Stargazer and patted the top. The mare, reliable as always, stood quietly. Summer gnawed her lower lip.

Teddy looked at Quinn, then the ladder. He still held the lead rope, sliding it between his fingers.

"Come on," Quinn said. "Time's a-wasting."

Seconds dragged into a full minute. Then, all at once, Teddy handed the lead rope to Quinn and climbed the stepladder as nimbly as if it was something he did every day. Throwing a leg over the saddle, he stuck his sneakered feet into the stirrups and gathered the reins.

Quinn half expected him to shout, "Giddyap."

"I… I don't believe it." Summer stared openmouthed. "Teddy, you're riding!"

"I've got to put this on." Quinn held up the harness and showed Teddy.

He lifted his arms, and Quinn did his best to attach the device without any fuss or unnecessary contact. Twice Teddy grunted and once he squealed. They did, however, eventually secure the harness.

"I'm shocked." A smile spread across Summer's face. "And impressed."

"Maw Maw. Ride." Teddy shook the reins.

"Yes, sweetie, I see you riding."

Quinn thought there might be tears in her eyes. He

longed to hug her again but resisted. A line crossed once was enough. To cross it again was out of the question.

"Where to?" He switched the lead rope to his other hand.

"Not the arena," Summer quickly responded. "It's enough he's on the horse. I'm afraid all the other riders and people will upset him."

"Okay. We'll use the small corral. It was empty a while ago."

"Thank you, Quinn."

The sincerity in her expression penetrated the shield he kept firmly in place around his heart. How was it possible she'd accomplished what only his family and his closest friends had?

They proceeded slowly down the aisle. Quinn held on to the lead rope, guiding the horse while Teddy rocked back and forth in the saddle, humming. Quinn had the impression it was out of enjoyment and not distress or fear. The tune reminded him of one he'd heard Summer sing to Teddy before.

Outside the stables, they went in the opposite direction of the arena. Summer changed sides, circling behind the horse to join Quinn. She glanced up at him and when he smiled, her features relaxed. Had she thought he wouldn't want her next to him?

Given his choice, he'd have her beside him in more places than the horse stables. Bed came to mind.

Wait, no, he couldn't let himself think like that. Then again, it was hard not to. She smelled great, looked fantastic and had felt incredible in his arms. More than anything, it was the affection in her eyes that captivated him.

"I still can't believe Teddy's riding," she said.

Quinn peered over his shoulder. Teddy appeared lost in his own world, seeing but not seeing. He also appeared content, as if the world he occupied was an enjoyable one. Knowing that wasn't always the case, Quinn was pleased for him and Summer, who also seemed content.

"I think the real test will be when it comes time to get him off the horse."

"You could well be right." She half sighed, half laughed. "Let's enjoy this part while it lasts."

Quinn entered the corral first, leading Stargazer. When all went without a hitch, Summer followed. The sun had begun its slow descent behind the McDowell Mountains, lighting the peaks while throwing the foothills into purple and gray shadows. Quinn didn't think he'd ever grow bored of the sight.

"Do you mind if I ask you a personal question?" he asked.

"Not at all." Summer smiled. "As long as I can reserve the right not to answer."

"Fair enough." Each trip around the small arena took only a few minutes. They were on their third one. "Given the chance, would you change your circumstances?"

"Circumstances?" Her smile dimmed. "You mean, would I want Teddy not to be autistic?"

"Not that. Would you still want to be married to Hal? Losing your family must have been difficult."

"Why do you want to know?"

"When I was in prison and learned Jenny had left the state, I told myself I didn't care and, eventually, I didn't. But that was when I had six more years left on my sentence. Lately, I've been thinking a lot about her. More specifically, what might have happened with the two of us if I wasn't arrested?"

"Are you still in love with her?"

"No. And not just because she left. Our relationship had run its course before the night in the bar and wouldn't have lasted much longer. But I wonder about Corrine and how I might have been part of her life all along if I hadn't gone to prison."

"Would you have stayed with Jenny, then?"

He liked that Summer didn't hesitate to ask him such direct questions.

"Hard to say. I was a different guy then. But I think yes. For Corrine's sake." He searched a little deeper and struggled with the feelings he uncovered. "I wish I didn't have regrets, but I do."

"Everyone does. And to answer your question, I wouldn't change circumstances. If Hal and I were still married, Teddy wouldn't be doing as well as he is. Hal has a different…opinion of autism. We didn't—don't—agree on a lot."

"I'm not defending him," Quinn said. "Don't take this wrong. But I understand how difficult it is when life doesn't turn out the way you planned."

"You're preaching to the choir."

"Yeah, sorry."

She gazed lovingly up at her son. "Then again, unexpected turns can also have wonderful results. Any difficulties with Teddy are far outnumbered by the rewards."

Quinn didn't consider himself the sentimental type, yet, for a moment, with Summer by his side, he was.

"It took a while for me to understand and accept that if Teddy wasn't autistic, Hal and I would probably still be married but not happy. One of those couples we all know who stay together because it's easier and less scary than starting all over with someone new." She absently patted Stargazer. "The pressure Teddy's disorder put on us was more than we could handle, and our marriage simply crumbled."

"I'm sorry."

"Don't be." She sniffed softly before visibly collecting herself. "I have to believe Teddy and I are where we're supposed to be."

"I'm waiting for that particular realization."

"Maybe you'll have it when you're reunited with Corrine."

Reunited. The word had a nice ring.

On their next circuit of the corral, a group of kids playing tag ran by. Quinn assumed they were siblings of the therapy program students. He'd seen them before. Perhaps bored and disinterested in watching the lesson, their parents had let them wander the grounds.

He might have ignored the kids except, on closer inspection, he spotted his nephew Nathan. Josh or Cara had to be nearby, but Quinn didn't see them.

"Just a sec," he told Summer. While she and Teddy waited, Quinn placed a call to his cousin Josh. "Hey, man. Where are you?"

"The ranch house."

"Look around. I think you're missing someone."

"No. Wait, am I?" There was a pause. "Yes, dammit. Nathan," he hollered.

"He can't hear you. He's here with us at the corral."

Josh swore softly under his breath. Twice. "Kimberly, put that down."

Quinn chuckled. Josh clearly had his hands full with his toddler daughter, which accounted for him losing track of his son.

"No worries. Nathan is here. He's playing with some of the other kids."

"I'll be right there." Josh uttered another curse under his breath. "Cara's going to skin me alive."

Nathan was a renowned escape artist. This wasn't the first time he'd evaded his parents' watchful eyes.

Quinn disconnected and pocketed his phone. As he did, the air was split by Nathan's cry of alarm. One of the other boys, considerably bigger and older than Nathan, had him pinned on the ground, a knee pressed into the center of his back, and was delivering a series of blows to his head. Nathan's cries increased.

"Hey!" Quinn yelled. "Knock it off." He looked at Summer.

"Go," she told him.

He ran out of the corral to where the boys were fighting. Without hesitating, he grabbed the larger boy by the waist and lifted him off Nathan. The boy kicked and yelled and flailed his arms, demanding to be put down.

Quinn obliged, setting the boy on his feet but keeping a firm grip on his shoulder so he wouldn't run off. The rest of the kids promptly scattered. "What's the problem?"

Nathan lifted his dirt- and tear-smeared face and, sobbing, said, "He h-hit m-me."

Red-faced and sweating, the kid spat out, "He stole my quarter."

"It's right there." Quinn bent and picked up the quarter.

Rather than be happy, the kid snatched the quarter from Quinn's hand and promptly kicked him in the shin.

Despite the sharp pain, he hung on to the boy's shoulder. "There's no need for that."

"Let me go."

"I will. Just cool your jets." He wanted to see if his nephew was all right. First, though, he needed to talk to this kid. "Trust me when I tell you, fighting's not the answer. It's especially wrong to pick on someone younger and smaller than you, even if he did take your quarter."

"Mom! Dad!" the kid yelled. "Help. He's hurting me."

"I am not." Quinn fought to keep his temper in check. It was one thing to defend yourself. Another to bully someone.

The kid abruptly twisted sideways, wrenched free and darted away toward the arena to join his friends.

"You okay, pal?" Quinn knelt and held Nathan tight. The boy buried his face in Quinn's neck, unable to stop crying.

"Poor little guy." Summer came over, leading Teddy and Stargazer. "Is he hurt?"

"Nothing serious from what I can tell." Quinn patted Nathan's back. "Come on, pal. Buck up."

The next moment, Josh came sprinting out from the direction of the ranch house. When Nathan spotted his father, his sobs turned into wails. Quinn handed over the boy while relaying what had happened.

"Thanks for intervening," Josh said.

"Glad I was here."

Nathan's crying jag finally subsided, and he held the back of his head. "Daddy, I have an owie."

Josh inspected the injured area, then Nathan's dirty face. "We'd better get you inside and cleaned up."

After they left, Summer laid a hand on Quinn's arm. "You're a good uncle."

"I might disagree. I wanted to throttle that kid."

"But you didn't."

"Right. Wish I'd shown the same kind of restraint three years ago."

"Maw Maw, man," Teddy called from atop Stargazer. "Ride."

They returned to the corral and made two more circuits. Quinn berated himself for not noticing Nathan's predicament sooner. As Summer's lively chatter and vivacious smile kept his attention focused on her, he cut himself some slack. It was a wonder he could put one foot in front of the other with her around.

Eventually, they returned to the hitching post outside the tack room. Here was the moment of truth.

"You ready to get down, son?" While Summer watched, and without any fuss from Teddy, Quinn unfastened the harness and set the stepladder next to the horse. "Okay, come on."

Teddy stared at the ground and sat motionless. Quinn expected him to start rocking and humming. He was about to reach for him when Teddy gingerly eased out of the saddle, swinging his right leg over and stepping down onto the ladder with his left.

"That's it," Quinn coaxed. "You're doing great."

Teddy lowered himself another step. Right before he reached the ground, he lost his balance and teetered precariously. Quinn caught Teddy by the arm and steadied him while he navigated the last step.

"There you go." He let go gradually and, without thinking, patted Teddy's back much like he had Nathan's.

Teddy went over to Stargazer's head and resumed stroking her nose. Quinn collapsed the stepladder and placed it out of the way. As he turned, he was taken off guard when Summer threw herself at him.

Not that he didn't like it, but he had to ask, "What's all this about?"

"Teddy let you touch him, and he didn't scream."

Quinn grinned, as much from Teddy's startling accomplishment as from holding Summer in his arms.

Chapter Six

There was no need for Quinn to walk her and Teddy to her car. Yet he had, and Summer relished the warmth blossoming inside her as he leaned in close to say goodbye.

They were standing at her open car door. Stargazer and the buckskin had been returned to their stalls, and Teddy was buckled into his booster seat. From the look of his drooping eyelids, he was ready to nod off. Another first. Teddy didn't sleep in the car. Not since he was in kindergarten—which was also the only time he'd attended public school.

"You haven't stopped smiling," Quinn said.

She touched her fingertips to her mouth and felt the curve of her lips. "It's been a good day."

The floodlights at the arena reached only to the fringes of the parking area, leaving Quinn and Summer cloaked in partial shadows. The lesson was ending. In another twenty minutes, the students would be finished with unsaddling their horses and, along with their families, making their way to their vehicles. Until then, and with Teddy nearly asleep, Summer and Quinn were relatively alone.

"You'll let me know when you hear more about your daughter?" she asked. Chances were she'd be updated at the office, except she'd rather talk to Quinn personally.

"You'll be my second call." He seemed pleased that she'd asked. "I promised the folks they'd be the first."

"They must be excited. Do they have other grandchildren?"

"Two. My older brother got married a few years ago. He has twin boys about Kimberly's age."

"And now they'll have a granddaughter."

"Another reason for everyone to spoil her rotten." Quinn somehow decreased the space separating him and Summer by several more millimeters.

She hadn't thought it possible as they were already close. "It's getting late. I have a mountain of laundry at home to fold and put away."

"See you tomorrow," he said as if tomorrow was much too long to wait to see her again.

She reached out and impulsively grabbed his arm, the fabric of his shirt bunching beneath her fingers. "Will you?"

He froze and locked eyes with her. "Count on it."

She swallowed. "Quinn, what's happening here?"

He stood impossibly still. "That depends entirely on you."

It was crazy and reckless and undeniably stupid. She could come up with a dozen different reasons off the top of her head to let go of him and hightail it away from the ranch.

Instead, she slipped her arms around his neck and whispered, "Kiss me."

His reaction was instantaneous. Circling her waist, he hauled her against him. Just at the moment his lips touched hers, he hesitated, perhaps giving her one last chance to come to her senses. Summer tightened her hold and, feeling instead as if she'd finally come to her senses for the first time in years, she kissed him hungrily.

It was, of course, incredible. *Just look at him, for cry-*

ing out loud. A man that sexy, that blatantly masculine, had been made to rock her world.

Angling her head, she arched into him, wanting to feel every possible inch where their bodies joined. Quinn groaned, low and with a desperation that let her know she mattered more to him in that moment than anyone else.

When his tongue swept into her mouth and they finally tasted each other, she sighed with satisfaction. This was how a man and woman should kiss.

Don't stop. Not yet. Make this last. Please.

Except, darn it, he didn't. Too soon, and with obvious reluctance, he broke off the kiss. She understood why. As much as she wanted to, they couldn't continue like they were. Not if they expected to walk away unscathed. Though, it would have been nice. Great. Fantastic.

He exhaled long and slow. "If things were different…"

"Yeah, I know."

"There's my daughter. And I have a record I'm trying to clear."

She nodded.

"There's also your ex-husband."

He'd listed three of the dozen reasons she had for not kissing him. "I shouldn't have—"

"Stop right there. This has been the best three minutes of my life since my release. We don't need to ruin it with a list of our mistakes."

He backed away from her car, but not before cupping her cheek and caressing her lips with the pad of his thumb. It was lovely, and she nearly pulled his head down for another scorching kiss.

Getting into the car, she told herself not to cry. What good would it do?

With a last wave, she shut the door and checked on Teddy—he was sound asleep—then pulled forward. At the end of the long driveway leading to the main road, she came upon a minivan just sitting there, red brake lights glowing in the dark. She recognized the vehicle—it belonged to a family whose son was a classmate of Teddy's. When had they left?

Summer suddenly panicked. Had the mother and her son finished early and spotted Summer and Quinn kissing? Was she waiting to confront Summer for acting inappropriately with an employee?

The driver's side door of the minivan opened and the mother emerged, her face illuminated by Summer's headlights. She motioned for Summer to roll down her window.

"There you are. I was just about to phone you."

Summer's anxiety escalated, though she acted nonchalant. "Hi, Mindy."

"Sorry about parking here." She motioned to her minivan. "I try not to call or text while I'm driving."

"It's a good habit to have." Summer's palms grew clammy. She glanced again at Teddy, who continued sleeping. At least she didn't have to worry about him hearing the conversation. "What's going on?"

"Have you met that new guy Cara hired for the therapy program?"

She must be referring to Quinn. "Yes."

"Then you've heard he's a convict."

"What I heard is that he was exonerated."

"That doesn't mean he's innocent."

"Actually, it does." Summer's relief was extremely short-lived. Mindy obviously hadn't seen the kiss. However, Summer didn't like the accusing tone in her voice.

"He worked the system," Mindy said. "Probably got a good attorney."

"It's my understanding new evidence was uncovered that cleared him. Another man was arrested. He took a plea agreement and is serving time. That amounts to admitting guilt."

Mindy braced her hands on Summer's open window. "This Crenshaw guy spent years in prison." She said *years* as if it was twenty and not two. "You can't possibly want that kind of person around our children."

Summer didn't want to give her and Quinn away. On the other hand, she felt an overwhelming need to defend him and not just because they'd kissed moments ago. In her opinion, right was right and wrong was wrong.

"I admit, I'm human and a parent. I would be cautious about a hardened, violent former convict working in close proximity to our children. But I also believe people can change and everyone deserves a fair chance. In Qu—" She caught herself before blurting his name. "In Mr. Crenshaw's case, he's innocent."

"And hardened. We've all heard about the terrible things that happen in prison."

"Have you met him?"

"Yes." Mindy lifted her chin.

"He's very nice."

"That could be an act. Jeffrey Dahmer's neighbors claimed he was a nice guy."

"Oh, Mindy." Summer couldn't hide her shock and horror. "Quinn Crenshaw is nothing like Jeffrey Dahmer. Please don't compare them."

Mindy backed away from Summer's car, her expression sour. "I've been talking to the other parents. They feel the same way I do."

"Really? All of them?" There were over thirty students in the therapy program.

"I'm still making calls," she said. "But the Gonzaleses agree with me. Also, Felicity Curtis."

Summer frowned. "Where's all this heading?"

"We're putting together a petition demanding Cara fire him."

"No." Summer gasped. "You can't be serious."

"One hundred percent."

"Why?"

Mindy made a sound of disgust. "Honestly, I can't believe your attitude."

Summer could easily say the same thing about her. "Tell me you'll think this through before you contact any more parents."

"I've thought plenty about it already." Mindy pushed at her hair as if the strands were the source of her irritation. "My mind's made up. This guy is bad news, and I refuse to allow him near our children."

She wouldn't allow it? Really? Well, Summer wouldn't allow this farce to continue a moment longer.

Opening the car door, she stepped out.

"Mindy." She waited until the other woman looked at her. "Your son has Tourette's syndrome."

"Yes." Mindy huffed, then demanded, "And?"

"Hasn't he been the object of teasing and pranks and tormenting from his schoolmates? Haven't you and your family suffered misunderstanding and—I hate to say it— prejudice from people who are ill-informed and ignorant about your son's condition?"

"Your point?" Her voice cracked when she spoke.

"Quinn Crenshaw deserves the same kind of treatment and tolerance from others as our sons do. As all people do."

"Our children aren't criminals."

"And neither is Quinn." Summer took a leap off the deep end. "You're a better person than this, Mindy. I've seen you fight for your son. Go toe-to-toe with the school administration and win them over with the sheer force of your convictions."

Mindy averted her gaze. Summer thought some of the fight might have gone out of her.

"Go home tonight, hug your child," she said, "and consider what I've said, okay?"

"I'm not making any promises."

"All right." She couldn't drag one out of Mindy if the woman wasn't ready. "I'll see you tomorrow?"

Even though she lived ten miles away, Mindy attended the same support group as Summer. "Fine."

On impulse, she pulled Mindy close. "We wouldn't be good parents and love our children if we didn't worry about them."

"I guess I am used to battling."

"Your family's lucky to have you."

Summer wanted to feel better after leaving the ranch, but she couldn't shake the concerns building inside her. Would Cara seriously consider a petition if things went that far? Should Summer mention the petition to Quinn and give him a heads-up or wait in the hopes Mindy reconsidered?

Mulling over the questions during the drive home and as she was putting Teddy to bed didn't provide any answers, other than affirming that she would do whatever was in her power to help Quinn and discourage Mindy from continuing with her petition.

QUINN SAT IN Marty's office, his hands gripping the visitor chair armrests and his right foot tapping nervously. It had been hard enough waiting a full twenty-four hours from Marty's initial phone call yesterday to this appointment. The last ten minutes had been grueling.

Summer had led him into the office, told him to sit and that Marty would join him shortly. That was—

He started at the sound of Marty coming in and shut-

ting the door behind him. Thank God. He'd been ready
to come unglued.

"How you doing, Quinn?" Marty sat behind his desk,
the leather chair creaking as he settled himself.

"Okay."

Truthfully, he'd been a wreck. Unable to eat, unable
to sleep and unable to concentrate. Growing increasingly
irritated with him, his cousins had insisted he take the
morning off work. Rather than ease his anxiety, Quinn had
spent the hours until the appointment alternately pacing
and searching the internet on his phone for articles about
ex-convicts getting shared custody of their children.

Marty cut to the chase. "I heard from the attorney we
hired in Seaside earlier."

Earlier! And he hadn't bothered to call Quinn? "What
did he say?"

"First off, he's not representing Jenny. He's simply acting as her messenger at our request. But be advised, she
will be retaining an attorney. Possibly one here in Arizona
to ease the process."

"Is that what she said?"

"Yes."

Quinn had expected as much. He'd sought legal counsel—
Jenny would, too. Nonetheless, it bothered him. Did she not
trust him to do right by Corrine?

"The good news is," Marty continued, "she's agreed to
bring your daughter here for a supervised visit."

Quinn's pulse jumped. "When?"

"The weekend of the sixteenth."

"Wait. No." He drew in a breath. "That's the same weekend as my cousin's wedding."

"Is it local?"

"Yeah. Mustang Valley."

"Good. You'll be available."

"I'll also be busy. I'm one of the groomsmen."

Marty tapped the screen on his electronic tablet, apparently reading his notes. "She wants to come on the sixteenth because it's her mother's birthday, and they're having a family party."

Anger surged inside Quinn. "My family's having a wedding. I think that trumps a birthday."

At Marty's frown, Quinn clamped his mouth shut and mentally counted to ten, then twenty. Losing his temper wouldn't advance his cause.

"I suggest you not start out making demands. Jenny's being reasonable, bringing your daughter here. Insisting she alter her plans might cause her to reconsider and dig in her heels."

"Alter her plans? She was already bringing Corrine here and not telling me."

"Remember, Quinn, she didn't know you were released."

She might have known if she hadn't run off and gone into hiding.

Rather than voice his feelings, he asked, "How am I supposed to spend time with Corrine when I have to go to a rehearsal dinner on Friday, the wedding and reception on Saturday and help clean up after the reception on Sunday?"

Marty's jaw visibly clenched but he remained calm. "Can't you find two hours each day? That's how long the visits will be. Friday afternoon, Saturday morning and Sunday morning. You might be able to pick up Jenny and Corrine at the airport, if that helps."

"Two hours? I thought I'd get to spend the whole day with Corrine."

"Frankly, you're lucky Jenny was already planning a trip to Arizona. Otherwise, you might not be seeing Corrine for weeks or even months."

"She kept my daughter from me all that time, and she can't give me one stinking day?" The hell with counting to twenty. Quinn was officially mad.

"Take it easy," Marty cautioned. "This isn't a battle you need to be fighting."

Little by little Quinn reined in his temper. It wasn't easy. Yes, Marty was right. That didn't make what he said easier to swallow.

Quinn tried to remember some of the things he'd read in the articles he'd researched. "Can she demand back child support?"

"Doubtful, since she didn't tell you about Corrine. Of course, she can ask for it now and likely will."

"I don't earn much."

"It might not hurt if you offered Jenny a share of your settlement from the state."

Quinn did take heart that Marty spoke with confidence, as if winning their suit against the state for wrongful conviction was a done deal.

"I'd be agreeable to that." Quinn didn't ask how much, assuming that would depend on the amount of the settlement. "Can I request that she and Corrine move back to Arizona?"

"You can't stipulate it." Marty shook his head. "But maybe she'll consider moving if you reach an amicable agreement. Her family does live in the Phoenix area."

"And if she doesn't move? How am I supposed to see Corrine? I can't afford to fly to Oregon more than once a year, if that."

"Let's cross that bridge when we come to it, okay? We start by asking for three-hour-a-day supervised visits rather than two, at a place of Jenny's choosing." Marty made entries on his tablet, seeming to be talking more to himself than Quinn. "One reasonable request sets the tone."

"Why does the visit have to be supervised? I'm not going to try to kidnap Corrine."

"That's not the only reason."

"She's my daughter. I would never hurt her."

"Supervised visits in the beginning are standard. Don't take it personally. In fact, don't take *any* of this personally. It'll only frustrate you."

"Is it because I was in prison?"

Marty grew impatient. "I said supervised visits are standard in the beginning. She needs to see you with Corrine. Feel confident you're good with her, and that she has nothing to worry about."

"She's kept my daughter from me for almost three years. Longer if you start counting from the time she got pregnant. I'm the one who's been wronged. Me and Corrine. Not Jenny."

"I understand your frustration. But there's a legal system in place we need to follow. Fighting her will only damage your case."

Quinn didn't think for one second that Marty understood his frustration.

"It's in your favor that you have a steady job and a stable home."

"I barely earn enough to put food on the table, and I live in an apartment over a horse barn."

Marty lowered his reading glasses in order to peer at Quinn. "Is it large enough for Corrine to stay with you?"

"Yeah. I suppose." He could always sleep on the sofa bed and give Corrine the bedroom.

"Really, Quinn. We're making progress. We located Jenny and Corrine quickly, and in a little over a week, you'll be seeing your daughter. That's what you need to focus on."

"Can Jenny refuse me shared custody?"

"Don't make trouble where there isn't any. And keep that temper of yours in check. Jenny already has enough ammunition to use against you."

"Like my record?" Quinn rubbed his temple, willing the ache there to abate.

"I'm just saying, don't give her any ideas."

They continued their meeting for another twenty minutes, finishing up when Summer sent Marty a message on his computer alerting him of his next appointment.

Marty stood and extended his hand to Quinn. "I'll be in touch as soon as I hear back from Jenny or her attorney regarding our request."

He escorted Quinn to the front office where a young couple sat, eyes nervously darting about. They sprang from their chairs the instant they saw Marty. Was everyone a wreck who came into his office?

Quinn noticed Summer wasn't at her desk. Where had she gone? Hadn't she just let Marty know of this couple's arrival?

He suppressed a stab of disappointment. Seeing her, if only briefly, would have given him a much needed lift, one he sorely needed after his meeting with Marty. Not that things had gone badly, he'd just hoped for more.

Taking the elevator, he stepped forward the instant the door swooshed open on the first floor—and nearly collided with Summer.

"Oops." She came to an abrupt halt.

Quinn took advantage of her surprise. Placing a hand on her shoulder, he guided her away from the elevator and the other two exiting occupants. "I was looking for you."

"You were?" She smiled. "I was in the parking lot meeting with the process server."

Behind them, the elevator doors closed. His earlier disappointment vanished when she didn't appear to regret missing her ride. Fortunately, the lobby was abandoned. Even so, Quinn pulled Summer along to a partially secluded nook behind a large planter.

"How'd the meeting go?" she asked. "You look happy."

Did he? He thought it might have more to do with running into her.

"Marty seems to think we're making progress." He shrugged.

"And you don't?"

"Jenny's bringing Corrine to Mustang Valley a week from Friday."

Summer's face lit up. "That's wonderful!"

"It's also the weekend of the wedding."

"Oh, you're right."

"And she only agreed to supervised visits. Two hours each day."

"But that's three visits over three days." Summer's smile returned. "You must be excited."

"I assumed I'd have Corrine all day."

"Marty's right," she assured him. "Things went well. Jenny could have said no. Run off again and gone into deeper hiding. Instead, she's being very accommodating and, frankly, I'm impressed. I was worried she'd give you grief and refuse to cooperate."

Somehow, it sounded better coming from Summer than Marty.

"I don't suppose you'd be willing to…"

"What, Quinn?"

"Hang around with me during Corrine's visit?"

She gave him a look. "You don't want me interfering."

"You wouldn't be." He exhaled. "I'm not sure how to behave with a little kid."

"You do pretty darn good with your niece and nephew."

"My future isn't on the line with them."

Summer shook her head. "Jenny may not appreciate my being there."

"I could use the moral support."

"Mmm… I'll think about it," she relented. "Maybe Teddy and I can just happen to show up an hour or so into your visit. If you don't need us, you can give me a sign."

"Thanks."

"I'm really pleased for you, Quinn." Her voice warmed. "You're going to be a terrific dad."

The impact of her joy for him was like an arrow to the heart. She hadn't merely given him a lift, she'd carried him straight up into the stratosphere. Unable to help himself, he drew her close for what he planned to be a quick kiss.

At first, she resisted. All right, the lobby of the building where she worked wasn't the best place to lock lips, even if the two of them weren't in plain sight. But he didn't let go of her and, slowly, she relaxed into his embrace.

For a minute, only one, they were lost in the kiss, and it was everything he remembered. Hot, hungry, exciting. Then Summer pulled away, sighing in a way that let him know she wished they were somewhere else. So did he.

"Sorry." Quinn was quick to apologize. "My timing could be better."

"That's not the reason."

"Right." There was no need to rehash their previous conversations. A romantic relationship was off-limits for both of them.

"It's complicated. In more ways than you realize." Her eyes misted. "I love seeing you and Teddy together. You can't imagine how I feel when I see him respond to you."

"I'm glad. He's a good kid, and I like him."

"I'm glad, too. But seriously, Quinn, can you imagine him as a permanent part of your life?"

"I haven't thought about it, to be honest."

"Right. Why would you? We're not to that point yet."

Yet? It cheered him that she wasn't ready to give up on them.

"If we were to get to that point sometime in the future," she continued, "you'd need to think long and hard about parenting a special-needs child. Teddy won't ever get better and may get worse."

"You said yourself he's making progress."

"At managing his disorder. Which improves the quality of his life and makes mine easier. But there's no cure."

"I know that, Summer." Quinn wanted to hold her again. He also doubted she'd allow it.

"Hal insists he wants more visits with Teddy. The sad truth is he can only handle an hour or two before he reaches his limit, and he's Teddy's father."

Quinn wondered if perhaps there was more going on than she admitted. "I realize Hal hurt you."

"And I don't want to be hurt again."

"No one does."

"The thing is," she said haltingly, "I have more than myself to worry about. There's Teddy. He's completely vulnerable, and I couldn't stand it if he were to suffer because I made a wrong decision."

"You and I aren't a wrong decision."

"Teddy's very fond of you. I can see it in his face. He rarely makes eye contact, and he does with you. What if you find out you can't cope with him? Not that I'd blame you. Eventually, we'd break up, you'd leave and Teddy would be devastated."

"I wouldn't just leave."

"Quinn, be realistic. You've been through some very difficult years, I grant you that. Nothing, however, has prepared you for parenting an autistic child. The hardships are intense and unending and can sometimes outweigh the rewards."

"I'm used to hardships."

"I know you mean well." She squared her shoulders. "I have to get back to work. Marty will be looking for me."

Quinn walked her to the elevator. "I care about you, Summer. A lot. And I won't give up on us that easily."

"I can't ask you to wait."

"What if I'm willing?"

"Quinn." She stopped and gazed fondly at him. "Whatever happens, promise me we'll still be friends."

Here it was. The dreaded let's-be-friends proposition.

Because she looked so forlorn standing there, he said "Absolutely," and pulled her against him for a hug, hoping against hope it wouldn't be their last.

Chapter Seven

Pacing didn't burn off any anxiety. Hadn't Quinn learned that in prison?

According to Jenny's last text message, they'd arrived at Sky Harbor Airport just before two. After a quick stop at her mother's to rest and borrow the car, they'd be on their way.

It was now three thirty. Quinn estimated they should be there any minute. Even then, they'd have less than two hours at most for this first visit. That was, if he hoped to make the wedding rehearsal in time.

Jenny had hired a local attorney, sending Quinn an email even before the attorney made contact with Marty. As yet, there'd been no discussion of child support, custody or DNA testing. Only the visits for this weekend. When, where and for how long.

Summer had suggested Quinn not bring up any sensitive topics and focus solely on getting to know his daughter. She was right, of course.

Not one of the texts or emails he and Jenny had exchanged this past week contained a picture of Corrine, though Quinn had asked for some. No matter. He'd take plenty this weekend to make up for it. His parents couldn't wait. They also wanted to video chat. Maybe tomorrow.

Jenny had conceded to a longer visit on Saturday in

order to compensate for today and Sunday being cut short. He planned on taking them to breakfast at the Cowboy Up Café sometime during the weekend, depending on how things went. Perhaps the park in town, as well. Summer had mentioned the playground area as a place where a three-year-old might have fun.

"Not here yet?" Raquel asked. She'd come into the living room while Quinn was staring out the large picture window.

"Shouldn't be long."

She patted him on the arm. "Try to relax."

"Easier said than done."

Gabe's mother was both matriarch of the Dempsey family and head of the household. Nearing sixty, she was pleasingly plump and still attractive. She frequently watched Josh's two kids while he and Cara worked and treated them as if they were her grandchildren even though they weren't technically related.

She'd also been kind to Quinn, going above and beyond to make him feel at home.

"For the *nina*?" She nodded at the stuffed purple pony Quinn held.

He set the pony on the coffee table. "Yeah."

Another of Summer's suggestions. Quinn had actually started a list.

"She will love it." Raquel smiled approvingly. "All little girls love horses."

"We'll see."

"I made some snacks. They're on the kitchen table. Cold drinks are in the refrigerator."

"You didn't have to, but thanks."

"You're welcome. I'm excited to have another young one in the house." She started to leave, then paused. "If you need anything, let me know."

He couldn't believe all Raquel had done to help him with Corrine's visit, considering the house was in a state of chaos. The party store had recently delivered rental tables and chairs for the wedding reception tomorrow. Friends and family members were readying the backyard, frantically erecting canopy tents, cleaning and decorating. Even some of the therapy program parents had volunteered to help. Raquel was in charge of the kitchen. Not trusting the caterers, she'd insisted on cooking the pulled beef and pork herself.

On impulse, Quinn went over and gave her a friendly hug. Not until that moment did he realize how much he missed his mother and the rest of his family. Weekly phone calls weren't enough.

"You're a sweet one." Raquel smiled kindly. "Someday, some lucky woman will figure that out."

Quinn's phone suddenly beeped, alerting him to yet another text message.

"I'll let you get that." Raquel padded away, returning to the kitchen.

Removing his phone from his pocket, Quinn checked the screen. The text was from Jenny. They were close.

The length of the living room was exactly twenty-one feet. He knew because he'd walked it at least that many times. He'd owe Raquel new carpeting after today to make up for the wear and tear he'd put on it.

Seeing an approaching car through the window, he tensed. For months, he'd imagined this moment. How he'd react, what he'd feel. Would he and Corrine have an instant connection? Recognize each other on some kind of instinctive level?

What if she feared or disliked him on sight? It was possible—she wasn't yet three. Did she even comprehend what was happening and who he was? How much had Jenny told her?

His stomach tied in vicious knots, he grabbed the stuffed pony off the coffee table and made his way outside.

Jenny parked in the driveway, following his instructions. By the time she shut off the car, Quinn was standing there, convinced his legs were about to give out. He hadn't been this nervous before any of his national championship rides. Not even when he faced G.I. Joe, the bull who reputedly held the record for breaking more cowboys' bones than any in history.

Jenny got out and smiled tentatively at him over the car roof. "Hi there. We made it."

Quinn forced his legs to obey his brain's signals and walked toward her. "Good to see you."

"Is it, or are you just being nice?"

Unsure if she was being funny or serious, he chose to ignore the question. "You made good time."

They stood face-to-face, the awkward moment stretching into two. Jenny was still attractive, her blue eyes vivid and her skin flawless. Once, a long time ago, she'd enticed her share of cowboys, Quinn included.

Now, as he studied her, he realized her looks left him lukewarm. He found Summer's beguiling hazel eyes and the smattering of freckles across her nose much prettier and much more to his liking. And that lush mouth of hers? Infinitely sexier.

He wanted her with him now, with an ache that surprised him. Hopefully, she'd show up later. Would it look bad if he called her in front of Jenny?

"How was the flight?" Quinn finally asked.

"Could have been worse. Corrine didn't cry a whole lot. Maybe she's getting used to it."

This took Quinn aback. "She's flown before?"

Jenny snapped her mouth shut as if realizing she'd revealed too much. "We've visited my mother before."

She traveled. Evidently a lot. It was on the tip of Quinn's tongue to ask if Jenny had ever wanted to see him in prison. Summer's words returned to him. *Don't bring up any sensitive topics.*

Instead, he asked, "Where's Corrine?"

"In the car." Jenny shut her door and opened the rear one.

Quinn caught a flash of movement and heard a small voice say, "Mommy, Mommy."

He inched closer and craned his neck to see into the backseat. A head covered in curly brown hair bobbed from side to side. Small hands reached up and grabbed Jenny. Quinn clutched the stuffed pony tighter.

All at once, Jenny straightened and stepped out from the open door, a beaming little girl in her arms. Quinn went still, his heart threatening to explode.

He wanted to say it was paternal love coursing through his veins, but that wouldn't be accurate. The feeling was more akin to wonder and fascination. He'd fathered a child. A strikingly beautiful one.

Corrine noticed him at last and stared with enormous dark eyes the same color as his.

"Wow" was all Quinn could manage to say, his throat having gone completely dry.

At the sound of his voice, she averted her head and buried her face in Jenny's shoulder.

"I know paternity testing is one of your requests," Jenny said, "but I can assure you, she's yours."

"I believe you." He swallowed. "Does she talk?" His nephew Nathan wasn't much older and talked up a storm.

"Yes. But she's shy around strangers."

A stranger? Was that what he was? He wouldn't be if things were different. If he hadn't gotten angry that night—

"And she's tired," Jenny added. "The traveling's disrupted her schedule."

Was that a hint they should keep their visit short?

"She's a beauty."

Jenny's smile went from tentative to glowing. "She is indeed."

"Can I see her? Hold her?"

And, like that, Jenny's smile disappeared. "Let's give her a few minutes."

Quinn clenched his teeth. He wouldn't argue. That was probably what Jenny expected of him. Instead, he'd show her he'd changed.

"Would you like a tour of the ranch? It's a little crazy around the house right now, what with the wedding tomorrow."

In reply, Jenny started walking the short road leading to the horse stables and corral.

"I'm glad for Josh. He had a real rough time with his first wife."

Jenny had known Josh through Quinn during their rodeo days. Those were also the days when Josh's wife had been deep in the grip of addiction.

"I forgot how hot it is here." Jenny paused and shifted Corrine to her other side.

When the little girl peeked out at Quinn over Jenny's shoulder, he flashed her a grin. She buried her face but not before giggling. A second later, she looked up, and Quinn held out the pony. Corrine's head shot up, and she reached out.

Jenny pivoted just as Corrine laughed, her small fingers gripping the pony's mane. She didn't appear happy.

"Well, say thank-you," she told Corrine.

The girl muttered it too softly for Quinn to hear. "You're welcome, honey."

Jenny frowned.

Did she disapprove of him giving Corrine a gift? "Let's check out the therapy horses. The stalls are shaded."

"I'm trying to picture you working with special-needs kids," she said when they continued walking. "Don't take this wrong, but it's not something I ever saw you doing."

"I actually work with the horses and not the students."

"You going back to the rodeo circuit?"

"No. Three years is a long time to be away. And besides being sorely out of practice, I'm not getting any younger."

"What plans *do* you have for the future?"

The question could be a casual one. Then again, she might be fishing for information. His answer could impact any agreement they came to regarding Corrine.

"I'm still getting my bearings," he finally answered. "It's only been a few months since my release."

"Sure, sure. But ultimately?"

She *was* fishing, he decided. "I like cattle ranching well enough and working with the horses."

"So, you're settling in Mustang Valley?"

"I'm willing to relocate and will if necessary. Whatever it takes to be near Corrine."

"Not much call for a ranch hand in Seaside."

"Your mother lives in Scottsdale. She must miss seeing you and Corrine."

Jenny visibly stiffened. "If you're proposing that I move, I have a job in Seaside." She hesitated. "And someone special."

He should have seen that coming. "Northern California is closer to Seaside than Arizona."

"Your grandparents' place?"

"Just tossing out ideas."

Quinn's grandfather had offered him a job the moment he was released. He owned one of the largest horse-breeding operations in the area. Quinn had turned him down, wanting a fresh start in a place where people didn't know him and his history.

He'd live there, however, if it enabled him to be closer to Corrine. Heck, he'd live on the far side of the moon.

The only problem would be leaving Summer. He didn't suppose it would be possible to have both her and Corrine—

"Mommy, horseys." Corrine lifted her free arm and pointed.

They'd reached the row of stalls where the therapy horses were housed. Jenny finally lowered Corrine to the ground. She immediately started forward, only to be held back by her mother.

"Be careful," Jenny warned. "Horses can hurt you."

Quinn thought it interesting how Jenny had changed. She used to be fearless. Motherhood must be responsible. Summer, Quinn had noticed, was also cautious with Teddy.

"Here," he said. "Let me."

Confident they had nothing to worry about with Mama, he grabbed Corrine under the arms and lifted her up, positioning her directly across from the gentle mare.

"No, Quinn!" Jenny tried to snatch his arm.

"It's okay."

Corrine squealed and wriggled for about three seconds, until Mama raised her nose and delicately sniffed her. Then Corrine burst into more giggles.

"The horsey kissed me."

"Her name is Mama," Quinn said.

"That's silly."

"Maybe a little."

She reached out and patted the mare's face. "Mama."

Quinn stared, mesmerized, the paternal love he'd wondered about earlier filling him.

How he wished Summer were here. She'd tell him being a father involved a whole lot more than adoring one's child, but he'd argue it was a start. And he did adore Corrine.

Oh, hell. Forget Summer's advice to steer clear of sensitive subjects. Quinn didn't want to communicate through attorneys. He was the kind of man who spoke for himself.

"Jenny, we need to talk. I'm going to do whatever it takes to make Corrine a permanent part of my life. She'll know who her father is and not just because he's someone who comes around once a year at Christmas or in the summer."

"Not now, Quinn."

"Then soon. Very soon."

Jenny's glance abruptly cut past him, and her frown returned.

Quinn pivoted to see Summer and Teddy appearing at the end of the stalls. They had Hurry Up with them, the small horse that belonged to Josh's son Nathan. Summer smiled at Corrine with unabashed delight.

"Who's she?" Jenny asked in a low voice. "And what's she doing here?"

"WELL, HELLO THERE!" Summer infused enthusiasm into her voice when she met up with Quinn, Corrine and Jenny.

She didn't have to work hard at it. Seeing a smiling Quinn holding the bubbly little girl filled her with relief. The visit was obviously going well. Father and daughter looked so natural and at ease together, Summer's spirits instantly soared.

Corrine gave her only a passing glance. She was much more interested in Teddy and stared intently, her features alight with curiosity.

That was why Summer loved young children. They didn't make snap judgments like adults. And if they noticed Teddy's differences, they either ignored them or accepted him like they would any other child.

"You must be Corrine." Summer moved closer to the little girl and Quinn. "I've heard a lot about you."

Jenny also moved closer.

Summer thought nothing of it. Mothers were instinctively guarded around people they didn't know, some more than others.

"And you must be Jenny," she said in an effort to put the other woman at ease. "It's nice to meet you."

"Same here."

When Jenny stood directly in front of Quinn, Summer reconsidered. Was something else going on she didn't know about? Like, perhaps, Jenny still harbored romantic feelings for Quinn. It wasn't outside the realm of possibilities and even made sense.

"Jenny, this is Summer Goodwyn and her son, Teddy." Quinn was slow making introductions, perhaps because he was enraptured with Corrine. Well, hard to blame him.

"Welcome to Dos Estrellas." Summer shook Jenny's hand.

"Thanks." Jenny glanced at Teddy. "Is your son a student in the therapy program?"

Realizing he was being talked about, Teddy became stressed. He dropped Hurry Up's lead rope and darted over to Quinn, where he crouched close and started humming.

"What's going on, pal?" Quinn patted Teddy's head reassuringly.

Summer bent to pick up the lead rope. If she didn't make a big deal of Teddy's behavior, hopefully no one else would, either.

"Teddy's in the program, but we're here today helping with the wedding preparations. Teddy needed a break from all the commotion, and we decided to take Hurry Up for a walk."

The ruse was a small one. Teddy had truly needed a break, but the idea to walk Hurry Up had been hers. It provided a means to accidentally-on-purpose run into Quinn and offer assistance if needed.

Fortunately, he and Corrine seemed to be getting along splendidly. Taking the girl to see Mama was a good idea. That, and the stuffed pony.

"Summer is Cara's maid of honor," Quinn said.

"Oh." Jenny raised her brows. "And, Quinn, you're the groomsman, right?"

"One of them."

An odd note colored Jenny's voice, giving more weight to Summer's jealousy theory. Then again, she didn't know Jenny. Perhaps it was best not to assume.

"This is Corrine." Quinn faced the little girl toward Summer. "My daugh—"

"No." Jenny immediately cut him off, going so far as to raise a hand as if to shield Corrine from danger. "I told you, she doesn't…know yet," Jenny finished in a whisper issued from the side of her mouth.

Quinn stiffened.

Okay, Summer thought. Not jealousy but unresolved issues.

"How do you like Mama?" she asked the girl, continuing her efforts at smoothing things over. "Isn't she pretty?"

"I like her." Corrine extended her hand toward the mare and wiggled her fingers. The mare nuzzled them, eliciting an excited squeak.

"This is Hurry Up." Summer presented the horse, who couldn't appear less interested. "He belongs to Nathan, your cousin—"

She stopped herself. Jenny probably wouldn't like that reference, either, and, as it happened, Summer was right.

"Corrine doesn't understand the complexities of family relations," Jenny stated tersely.

Quinn expelled a subtle, yet discernable, sigh of frustration.

Summer felt bad. She'd only made things worse for him. "Well, Teddy and I should get going and let you finish your visit. I guarantee you're in good hands with Mama," she assured Jenny.

"Stay," Quinn offered.

Um, yeah. She'd be as welcome as a skunk at a birthday party. "I'm sure Raquel could use some help in the kitchen."

"I promised Corrine a horse ride." Quinn was already on the move and took the lead rope from Summer. "We can saddle this fellow quicker than we can Mama. Plus, he's smaller. You coming with us, Teddy?"

"No," Jenny protested, once more raising her hand. "She's too young to ride."

"Nathan rides Hurry Up all the time, and he's only a little older than Corrine."

Summer observed the power struggle between Quinn and Jenny. She wanted to tell him to back off. He wouldn't win any points with Jenny or make their future custody discussions proceed any more easily if he exerted himself this early on.

Now, however, wasn't the time. "Come on, sweetie." She motioned to Teddy.

Her son had other ideas and grabbed on to Quinn's belt loop with a grip that left no doubt he intended to remain put. Summer wasn't inclined to engage him in front of Jenny. He'd had a tough day and would likely pitch a fit.

Which meant they were stuck where they were for the immediate duration. Shoot.

Together, they started for the horse stables and the tack room at its center. Jenny clearly wasn't happy, but she, too, chose to forgo a battle. Summer respected her for making the right decision. It couldn't have been easy.

Inside the stables, she engaged Jenny in small talk while Quinn saddled the horse. Teddy stayed by his side and shadowed his every step. Quinn, as usual, didn't mind. With luck, Jenny might notice.

When Corrine was returned to her and safely nestled in her arms, Jenny appeared to relax. The three of them stood to the side while Quinn groomed Hurry Up.

"I heard it's your mother's birthday," Summer said.

That drew a surprised look from Jenny. "Did Quinn tell you?"

"Um, yes."

"You two are good friends, then?"

"We're friends." Summer deftly changed the subject. "He's great with Teddy, as you can see. He's good with all the therapy program children."

"He told me he doesn't work with them."

"Yes, but he's around, and they've taken to him." Summer thought of Lizzie, the student with Down syndrome. "Nathan and Kimberly adore him."

Was she overselling Quinn? She bit her lower lip and took a mental step back.

"Never thought I'd see the day." Jenny bounced Corrine in her arms. The little girl wanted to be on the ground with Teddy and petting Hurry Up's nose. "Quinn didn't have the least interest in kids when we dated."

Was that another reason she'd gone into hiding when she discovered she was pregnant? Concern that Quinn wouldn't want their child?

"People do change," Summer said. "You haven't seen him in a while."

Jenny's gaze narrowed. "Exactly how much did he tell you about us?"

"Only a little." Summer glanced at Quinn to divert attention away from herself.

He'd retrieved a child's saddle from the tack room and was now putting the bridle on Hurry Up.

"We can use the arena," he said, checking the girth and taking it in another notch. "It's empty."

Once more, they traveled together as a group, Teddy on one side of Quinn, Jenny on the other. Summer followed behind. She told herself she didn't mind, except she did. Kind of.

At the arena, she waited while Quinn lifted Corrine onto the small horse. Arms high in the air, she laughed with excitement, not at all afraid. Evidently, she took after her father when it came to riding horses.

"Do you mind getting some pictures?" Quinn asked Summer.

"Not at all." She reached for her phone.

"You can send them to me later."

With Jenny giving her more strange looks, Summer clicked shot after shot of Quinn leading Corrine on Hurry Up around the arena. Teddy had gone with them and walked beside Quinn. A few weeks ago, Summer would have been shocked. Today, she accepted Quinn and Teddy's friendship as the norm.

People could indeed change, she mused while snapping a close-up of Teddy looking up at Quinn.

She insisted on excusing herself and Teddy a short while later. Quinn needed time alone with his daughter and Jenny. Plus, Summer had committed to helping with the wedding preparations.

"Come on, sweetie. Mommy's got things to do." She braced herself for Teddy's refusal.

Hooray, hooray, he complied without much fuss.

Quinn patted him lightly on the back and said, "See you later, son."

When Corrine waved and uttered a sweet, soft "Bye," Summer felt a strong tug on her heart.

Please let this visit end well for Quinn.

At the house, she joined the crew of helpers in the backyard. That way, she could watch Teddy, who played with one of the ranch dogs. Holding a stick, he ran in circles while the dog chased him and barked. It was a similar game to one he played with their own dog, Paw Paw.

Other children were also there, creating chaos whenever possible. Nathan, with his remote-controlled truck, was the center of attention. Among the group of six surrounding him were several of the therapy program students. Summer was glad to see Nathan made no distinction when it came to playmates, treating them alike regardless of their disabilities.

She was mostly glad to see the therapy program parents and took their willingness to help as reassurance nothing had come of Mindy's campaign to have Quinn fired.

As she and the others worked, the sun beat down relentlessly, making their tasks that much harder to accomplish.

"Whew, it's hot," Summer said to no one in particular, wiping her damp brow with the back of her hand. With the other, she steadied a crepe paper–covered arch.

Gabe knelt at the base of the arch, driving stakes into the ground to anchor it. By early tomorrow evening, a four-tier wedding cake would be placed on a table beneath the arch and the happy couple would be smashing small pieces into each other's faces.

"Remind me to talk to Josh about the weather." Gabe

stood and stretched. "He and Cara picked a heck of a time to get married. Didn't anyone tell them the humidity's at a record high?"

Summer didn't think Josh and Cara cared. They were ready and eager to start their lives together.

She envied her friend. At one time, she'd been like Cara, hopeful and excited about what the future held. Would she ever feel like that again?

"Uncle Quinn!" Nathan flew past them at a dead run. "Where's Hurry Up?"

Quinn ambled nearer, Jenny and Corrine noticeably absent. They must have returned to their car, and Summer had been too busy to notice.

"I put him back in his stall." Quinn stooped to gather Nathan in his arms and swung him around.

"Take me riding," Nathan insisted.

"Sorry. Can't. We've got a lot of work here, and then there's the wedding rehearsal. Are you and your sister ready?"

Nathan pouted. He and Kimberly had been recruited for ring bearer and flower girl. Neither of them was taking their job seriously.

"What if we saddle Hurry Up and a couple of the other horses tomorrow at the reception? Keep you and your friends busy and out of trouble?"

"I'm being good," the boy announced proudly. "I'm sharing my truck and my horse."

"Yes, you are, and I appreciate it." Quinn sought out Summer's gaze and, when he found it, smiled.

"How'd the rest of your visit go?" she asked.

"Well. Better than expected."

The warm glow she'd experienced when he first glanced at her increased. She could easily go on looking at him indefinitely.

Unfortunately, it wasn't in the cards. Nathan chose that moment to insist on rejoining his friends.

"Hold on a second." Quinn didn't release the boy until he had both feet planted firmly on the ground.

Nathan started running—only to stop a short distance away and begin howling at the top of his lungs.

"What's wrong?" Quinn hurried toward him, as did Summer and Gabe. Quinn reached Nathan first.

"My foot!" The boy fell onto the ground and grabbed his left sneaker. Rocking back and forth much like Teddy did, he began to sob. "It hurts."

"Let me see." Quinn took hold of Nathan's foot and tried to examine it.

Nathan rolled onto his side and wrenched his foot free. "Nooooo!"

From where Summer stood, she had a better angle and spotted the problem. "There's a nail sticking out of the sole."

"You've got to hold still, pal." Quinn gripped Nathan's ankle firmly in his strong hands. Eventually, he quieted.

The nail wasn't large and probably hadn't penetrated deep. Nonetheless, it must have pricked Nathan enough to cause some pain.

"What can I do?" Summer asked.

By now, a small audience had gathered and even people from other parts of the yard were watching them.

"Someone dropped a nail," Gabe said, glancing around for more. "It was bound to happen."

People had been using nails all day to hang decorations on the patio, fence and even the tree in the center of the yard.

"One more second," Quinn said.

"Ow!" Nathan complained. "You're hurting me."

"I'm trying not to."

Summer suspected a large part of Nathan's outburst was due to fear. Quinn was exceedingly patient and finally managed to yank off the sneaker.

The embedded nail was indeed small. Summer retrieved the sneaker and removed it. Nathan continued to make a fuss while Quinn peeled off his sock and inspected his bare foot.

"I think you'll live," Quinn pronounced.

"A washing and bandage is probably in order," she added.

Nathan flung himself onto his back. "I want Daddy."

"He and Cara are running an errand." They'd gone into Scottsdale to obtain the marriage license. "What if I give you a hug? Will that help?"

Summer opened her arms. Nathan jumped up and threw himself at her. She lowered herself to his level and squeezed tight. It felt wonderful to hold a young child, and she had trouble letting go even when Nathan, miraculously healed, squirmed to get free.

"Not before you put your sock and shoe back on," she admonished.

She barely got the Velcro strap fastened before Nathan broke into fresh sobs and ran away.

"Daddy, Daddy!" he cried out. "I got hurt."

Josh and Cara, it seemed, had arrived home.

Summer straightened and gave a laugh. "He's a bigger drama queen than his sister."

Quinn shook his head. "The good thing is he's all right."

"Yes." She waited a moment until their audience had dispersed. "Want to tell me about your visit with Corrine while I sort flowers?"

"Sure."

They strolled over to the back patio and the large box of crepe-paper flowers, handcrafted by the bridesmaids over the past week. Summer made sure Teddy was all right. He'd abandoned the dog to its stick in favor of watching the other children play—from a distance, naturally. At least he was watching them, she thought, and not ignoring them.

Summer also couldn't help noticing the stares she and Quinn garnered. Most were friendly. Two or three from some of the therapy student parents, though, were decidedly cool.

Summer went still. So much for assuming she'd convinced Mindy to abandon her plan. Did Cara know? What if Mindy actually succeeded and got Quinn fired?

A heavy sensation in the pit of Summer's stomach lingered until Cara announced it was time to leave for the rehearsal at the church. After that, Summer was too preoccupied to think of anything else.

Chapter Eight

Of the two hundred plus guests at the wedding reception, less than fifty remained. Most of them were family and friends, recruited to help with shutting down the celebration and general cleanup.

Summer carted an empty chafing dish into the kitchen, strains of country music following her inside. The four-piece band regularly performed at the Poco Dinero Saloon in town and had given the Dempseys a good price, throwing in an extra hour of playing time for the bride and groom. At this hour, few couples were dancing. Still, the band continued to entertain.

Speaking of the bride and groom, they'd left a short while ago to embark on their honeymoon. For tonight, they were staying at the Talking Stick Resort. Tomorrow morning, they'd drive to Pinetop for a secluded four-day stay in a friend's cabin. They'd left strict instructions not to be disturbed except for emergencies.

Though the bride and groom had been the center of attention at the reception, Cole and Violet's recent elopement was also toasted, and the stacks of presents piled in the living room included many for them, as well.

Raquel had agreed to watch Nathan and Kimberly during the five days their parents would be out of town and was at this moment attempting to coax them to sleep in one of the empty bedrooms. The excitement of the day had sent them into hyperdrive rather than wearing them out. Summer had decided to oversee the dinner cleanup while Raquel was occupied with the children, and several people had volunteered to assist her.

It had been a beautiful wedding and gone off without a hitch. Summer's heart stirred as she recalled Josh and Cara reciting their personally written emotional vows. The children had been adorable and managed to get through the ceremony—barely. The bride had been stunning, her carefully chosen dress flattering her advancing pregnancy rather than hiding it, and the groom was handsome in his tux.

The groomsmen weren't half-bad-looking, either. All right, they were gorgeous. One in particular. Summer hadn't been able to take her eyes off Quinn the entire time, to the point she was afraid of drawing unwanted attention.

They'd been placed together several times during the photo sessions at both the church and the ranch. Summer had gone weak in the knees being near him, all her self-warnings these past weeks going by the wayside. She was still smitten with him, if not on the verge of something greater.

Better she keep busy with the cleanup before she dropped a pan or broke a platter. Stepping outside again after another trip to the kitchen, she glanced around for Quinn. Come to think of it, she hadn't seen him for a while now.

As promised, he'd saddled up a couple of the gentler horses and supervised rides for the children in attendance. About an hour ago, with people beginning to leave, he'd returned the two horses to their stalls. She'd spotted him once after that, but not for a while now.

What was he doing? Had he retired to the apartment?

The next instant, she saw him talking to Cole in a corner of the yard and pretended the fluttering in her stomach was residual excitement from the wedding.

Singing softly to herself—she'd always liked this particular song the band was playing—she made her way to the long line of tables that had held food and currently looked like a war zone.

Out of habit, she searched for Teddy. Silly—he wasn't there. She'd missed him during the reception and would have liked him to attend but was glad she'd decided to leave him at his favorite sitter's for the night. This would be his first time sleeping over at the sitter's house. Another milestone reached.

Summer had checked her phone often during the evening and placed two calls to the sitter. According to the last report, he'd gone willingly to bed. Taking their dog, Paw Paw, to the sitter's, along with several beloved toys and his favorite pajamas, had probably helped keep him calm.

This was, she realized, the first time she'd be away from Teddy in over four years. Since well before his diagnosis. Knowing he was in good hands allowed her to relax. She might even indulge in a glass of wine and a bubble bath when she got home, a treat she denied herself and something she deserved after the long day.

Standing at the table, she heard movement behind her and sensed the presence of someone approaching. The next instant, she inhaled a familiar aftershave. It was the same one that had invaded her dreams repeatedly of late.

"Why don't you put that down," Quinn said, "and let's dance."

She turned slowly and took in the sight of him. He'd done away with his tux jacket at some point, along with his cummerbund, bolo tie and brand-new cowboy hat. The slightly rumpled appearance suited him, and her knees went weak all over again. Could she even dance?

"I really should—"

He didn't let her finish and, instead, took her by the hand, leading her to the area in front of the band that had been reserved for dancing. They were the only ones.

With an ease she found incredibly sexy, he pulled her into his embrace and fit her comfortably to him as if they'd danced together many times rather than never before. She'd imagined this moment often during the reception, seeing other couples locked together and swaying to the music. But he hadn't asked her, and she'd been too shy to ask him. She'd spotted him several times on the dance floor, once with Violet, another time with Cara's mother and later with a few women she didn't know.

She, of course, had danced with Cole. Wasn't that practically a requirement for the best man and maid of honor? Also Cara's father. Neither time had been as wonderful as this. Quinn held her tight, even possessively. She didn't object. In fact, when he smoothly turned her in a half circle, she held on more securely, never wanting the music to end.

He leaned down, put his mouth close to her ear and said, "Sorry for the completely unoriginal line, but you look great tonight."

"Thanks." It had been a long while since Summer felt attractive. The pale yellow taffeta dress was quite lovely, and her reflection in the mirror had pleased her, though it hadn't made her feel half as good as Quinn's remark. "I might say the same about you."

"'Fraid I couldn't stand to wear that jacket a minute longer. Damn thing is stifling."

"Well, there are always the pictures to remember us by." She'd be sure to request several copies for herself.

Though no one joined them on the makeshift dance

floor, the band continued with another slow number. Summer figured this had to be their last and decided to enjoy herself while she could.

"What time is Jenny bringing Corrine by tomorrow?" she asked.

"Early. Their flight leaves at two. I offered to meet them at a halfway point, but Jenny said Corrine loves the horses. Can't say I'm not glad she inherited at least one thing from me."

Summer didn't mention Jenny's earlier reservations about Corrine riding and instead asked, "Everything go as well today as it did yesterday?"

With all the hustle and bustle surrounding the wedding and reception, she hadn't found a free moment to talk with him about the visit.

"It went great, if a little rushed. Jenny left early. She claimed Corrine was tired." He sounded as if he didn't quite believe Jenny.

"She's still young. Children her age typically nap every day."

"Jenny did leave me alone with Corrine for a whole ten minutes."

The hint of amusement in his voice was nice to hear. At least he wasn't angry anymore about the supervised part of their visits. "You can laugh, but it's a start."

"Marty suggested I talk visitation with Jenny tomorrow."

"Really?"

"He wants me to try to get a sense of what she's willing to do."

Summer couldn't help but notice his muscles tightening. "You nervous about that?"

"I don't want this to turn into open warfare. But with

her living in Oregon and not likely to move back here, it might."

Summer took a deep breath. "You could always move."

Though she had no right whatsoever to ask, and would never deny Quinn the opportunity to be with his daughter, she selfishly wanted him to remain in Mustang Valley.

"I doubt it. There's not much work for me in or near Seaside. I checked online. It's mostly a beach town. Besides, I probably need to be here, for a while at least. As long as Marty's willing to work my case against the state pro bono."

He clearly needed to talk, and she wanted to be the one he chose to confide in. Except she missed the thrill when he'd been entirely focused on her and their dancing.

"You have to remain optimistic," she said. "That's the only way you'll get through this. Jenny has reasons to visit Arizona, what with her mother living in the area. And you can go there. There are also the summer months. A lot of fathers take their children during school breaks."

Quinn moved his hand from Summer's waist to the center of her back. The few inches magically increased their intimacy, and she was once again dizzy from his touch.

"Four months ago, I couldn't imagine myself as a father. Now that I am, now that I've met Corrine, I know I don't want to do this part-time. 'Course, there's no chance in hell Jenny would agree to give me custody."

"I understand how you feel. I see it a lot at work. There are fathers who want nothing more than to be involved in their children's lives and can't because of circumstances like distance or jobs. Then there are the fathers who have the ability but don't give a hoot about their children. It's not always fair."

"Is Hal still insisting on seeing Teddy more often?"

Quinn must have been reading her mind. "In fact, when

he learned I called the sitter for today, he insisted on taking Teddy. I debated long and hard about letting him and finally agreed. I wanted to find out if his motives were genuine. Then he called me this morning and backed out. I'm lucky the sitter was available."

"Are you surprised he did?"

"I wish I was. He now says he wants to see Teddy in the morning and that he's going to pick up him up from the sitter's. We'll see." She shrugged one shoulder.

"Has he mentioned me again?" The strain in Quinn's voice was obvious even over the sound of the band playing.

"I've been careful about going to the market only when the manager isn't there. I don't want to give him a chance to gossip about me again."

"You didn't answer my question."

"He might have," she relented.

"Summer."

Quinn looked around as if to see whether they were being watched or not. For some reason, that annoyed Summer.

"Relax. Hal doesn't have the right to dictate who I dance with or who I see."

Quinn allowed a lazy grin turn his mouth up at the corners. "Am I hearing you right? Are we going to start seeing each other?"

"You know we can't. And Hal isn't the only reason." If only that weren't true. Summer swore she could feel her heart breaking.

This time, when the band stopped playing, they quit for the night. The lead singer thanked the remaining audience, and the members began to disassemble.

"Come on." Quinn took her hand again. "I'll help you clean up."

"You sure? You have to get up early tomorrow."

"And when we're done here, I'll drive you home. Violet mentioned she picked you up on the way to the church."

"That's not necessary, Quinn."

"No arguing."

She didn't. Having Quinn drive her home was infinitely more appealing than even that glass of wine and bubble bath she'd been contemplating.

"YOU TIRED?" QUINN ASKED.

"Yes…and no." Summer gazed out the passenger window at streetlights and dimly lit landmarks. They were nearing her house. Quinn had never been there and needed directions. "It's been a long day. A long month. Weddings are a lot of work. But I'm excited for both Cara and Josh and Cole and Violet." She took a moment to marvel at the recent changes. "Do you realize there will be two babies born less than five months apart? The Dempsey family is certainly growing."

"I hadn't thought about it."

Of course not. He was a guy, after all. A rough-and-tumble kind of guy with hard edges and a love of adventure. The kind who rode bulls and busted broncs for a living or ran cattle. Someone else's babies weren't particularly interesting.

She, on the other hand, found *him* interesting and was confident he shared her feelings. She needed only to recall their kisses and the way he'd held her tonight while they danced …

Sitting up straighter, she indicated the next road. "Turn right here, then right again."

"What brought you to Mustang Valley?"

Huh? How did he know she wasn't from this area? Had he asked around?

"Hal. His father moved the Goodwyn family here, oh,

during the seventies, I suppose." She had to think about it. "He was a park ranger up until he retired. Thirty-five years with the federal government."

"How did you and Hal meet?"

"My old college roommate introduced us. I was going through a rough patch. First, I was laid off from my job, then my boyfriend dumped me."

"Ouch."

"My friend invited me here over Memorial Day weekend in the hopes of cheering me up. She happened to be dating Hal's coworker. He and I hit it off, and when he suggested I stick around another week, I did."

"Ah, a rebound romance?"

"It's kind of true, I suppose, though I did make Hal wait three years before I married him just to be sure. I started looking for a job that first weekend and, by some stroke of luck, landed one at Marty's." She tapped her chin. "Which I guess means I've been with Marty longer than I was with Hal."

The thought was a little unsettling, and she was glad the truck's dark interior hid her reaction.

"This is it." She sat up and pointed. "Second house from the corner."

He pulled into the double-wide driveway and parked in front of the closed garage door. She observed him taking in the Sante Fe–style exterior, red tile roof, enclosed courtyard and attractive desert landscaping.

"Nice." His tone reflected his appreciation.

"I like it. The backyard is huge and one of the reasons I chose the house. Plenty of room for Teddy to play."

He got out of the truck and came around to her side. By the time he reached her, she was already getting out. Not that Summer was a hardcore feminist like her mother, but she and Quinn weren't on a date, and she'd rather not send the wrong signals.

"Looks new," Quinn remarked as they made their way to the front door. Twin potted plants flanked the front door, and a trio of terra cotta quail formed a small parade along the walkway.

"Mustang Valley's newest neighborhood," Summer said, letting her pride show.

"I assumed you'd lived here with Hal."

They stopped at the door, and Summer searched her purse for her key. "No. I bought the house. Teddy and I lived in duplex after the divorce. I wanted something bigger."

She wondered what would happen next. Would Quinn leave? Shake her hand or kiss her good-night? She debated inviting him in, but there were those mixed signals she vowed to avoid.

"Thanks for driving me home," she finally said.

"Call me tomorrow if you need anything."

Okay, he was planning on leaving. Why, then, wasn't she relieved? "I'm not sure what time I'll be at the ranch for the big cleanup. It depends on when Hal picks up Teddy and decides he's had enough." Summer sent Quinn a guilty look. "Oops. That wasn't very nice of me."

He grinned in a way that had her heart skipping erratically. "I won't tell."

"I'll deny it if you do."

That earned her a chuckle.

Darn it, did he have to look so sexy in the glow of the porch light? The shadows emphasized his strong, compelling features and lent him a romantic and mysterious appearance. He could have starred in one of those late-night classic films from the fifties, giving James Dean or Clark Gable a run for their money.

That, she supposed, would make her the ingenue. Her imagination immediately took flight.

"I'd love to know what you're thinking right now."

A low, rumbling voice interrupted her thoughts and sent shivers of the good variety skittering along her spine.

"You would?" She stared up at him, certain he could hear her wildly drumming pulse.

Removing his cowboy hat, he leaned down and touched his forehead to hers. His arm felt strong around her waist as he anchored her to him.

"Unless you tell me no, I'm going to kiss you, Summer."

Tell him no? Was he joking?

"Yes. Please."

When he moved to make good his promise, she stopped him with a hand centered on his chest. He drew back, surprise registering on his face. Well, she had practically begged him to kiss her.

"Not here." She stood on tiptoes and brought her mouth close to his. "Inside."

His eyes widened, then glinted with desire. "Yes, ma'am."

Turning, she inserted her key in the lock and opened the door. Convinced he would follow her, she nonetheless smiled to herself when she heard the sound of his boots on the ceramic tile.

Where this was leading, Summer had no idea. She knew only that she wanted to be with Quinn. For a while, at least. She also wanted to feel sexy and desirable and even a little decadent. Was that so wrong?

A sudden gentle pressure on her arm stayed her.

"Here?" Quinn asked, lowering his head. They stood in the entryway, directly beneath the overhead light.

"No. Not yet." She stepped away from him.

He resisted and held on to her.

She slid out of his grip and, taking his hand, led him across the living room to the hallway where a dim wall sconce provided the perfect amount of illumination, enhancing rather than ruining the mood.

"Now?" he asked, pushing her hair off her neck and placing his lips on the patch of bare skin just above her collarbone.

"Quinn." His name came out on a soft sigh.

"Should I stop?"

"You do and I swear I'll never speak to you again."

"You're hard to resist, Summer." There was a raw edge to his voice as his mouth climbed the side of her neck.

"Nothing worthwhile is easy."

Before she quite realized what was happening, he pushed her up against the wall, pinning her between him and the unyielding surface.

"What are you doing?" As if she didn't know.

"Whatever you want, darling." He nuzzled her ear, then nipped delicately on her sensitive lobe before taking it between his teeth. "My next move is entirely up to you."

Advance and retreat, only to advance again. It was a titillating combination, and every nerve in her body hummed in delicious response.

"No kiss first?" She tilted her head to give him better access to her neck, not quite ready to quit the game.

He got the message loud and clear. Pressing his lips to the skin just below her jaw, he traced a silky line with his tongue. "I'll get around to it eventually."

"Don't let me hurry you."

A sound of both despair and urgency came from deep in his chest, echoing her own desires. She hadn't been with a man in ages. Even so, it wasn't her dry spell that fueled the hunger building inside her. She wanted Quinn and only him.

He held her close, his wanting of her undeniable. Nudging her legs apart, he murmured, "You have no idea how often I've thought about you in exactly this situation."

Her. Not just anyone. She alone was the center of his fantasies.

"Tell me about it."

His chuckle was low and brimming with humor. "You want details?"

"Actually, I think I do."

"Mmm." His smile spread wide across his face. "Tempting."

"Are you going to rock my world, Quinn?"

"I'd like to try."

"What about all the reasons we should wait? Steer clear of each other?" She was the one, after all, who'd kept insisting their timing was off.

"Those haven't changed." He lowered his voice. "What has is us and our feelings for each other."

He was right. What did being cautious really get them? A life without experiencing the exquisite touch of one's lover? The enjoyment of waking up snuggled next to a warm, giving body? Summer had gone too long without those things and missed them.

"What if I say no?" she asked, not yet ready to commit. "Can we still be friends?"

"The best of friends."

"And if I say yes, and it turns out to be only one night?"

"Still friends. I don't quit and run at the first sign of trouble."

Her throat suddenly closed as emotions consumed her. "Quinn."

He took her in his arms and placed a chaste kiss on her forehead. "It's okay, darling. Send me away if you're not ready. I won't force myself on you."

"No, no. I want you to stay. I just need to be absolutely sure. Can you understand? There's a lot riding on this."

He slid the fingers of his right hand into her hair and cupped the back of her head. Firmly and decisively and yet tenderly. Or maybe it was the look in his eyes that melted her heart. "I want to make you happy. I think I can. God knows, I'd like to try. But it's up to you."

Insisting he leave would be a lot easier if he weren't such a perfect gentleman.

"How about that kiss first?"

"My pleasure." He drew her into his embrace and covered her mouth with his.

They started gentle and slow, then quickly gained momentum. Summer didn't resist when his tongue swept into her mouth, didn't protest when his hands slid lower to grab her hips and align them with his, and didn't dare think of objecting when he pressed the hard line of his erection into the junction of her legs.

In fact, were she capable of talking, she'd encourage him to be bolder, take greater liberties and push more boundaries. There might never be another time like this again in her life, and she'd be a fool not to make the most of it.

Drawing on her last ounce of strength, she ended the kiss and retreated a step. Acceptance showed in Quinn's dark eyes, and he nodded, ready to end their evening.

She had a surprise in store for him.

Slipping away, she turned toward the hall leading to the master bedroom, moving with what she hoped was her best seductive walk.

"Are you coming with me or not?"

Chapter Nine

Quinn woke slowly, stretched and stifled a yawn. Red digital numbers on the nearby alarm clock announced the time: 6:14 a.m. He mentally counted and groaned. Five hours wasn't enough sleep. Yet, he wouldn't change a single thing about the previous night. It had been that incredible.

Beside him, Summer stirred.

"Shh." He brushed a stray lock of hair from her forehead, resisting the urge to kiss the spot he'd exposed. "Go back to sleep."

The sun peeked through the plantation shutters covering the bedroom windows. It was well past Quinn's normal rising time; he'd usually showered, dressed and was heading down the apartment stairs by now.

Today he dallied, the lure of Summer's warm, naked body difficult to resist.

Besides, this might be their one and only time. They'd talked a lot during the long hours together but not about the future. Better he savored every moment and remembered every detail.

"I have to get up," she said sleepily as she snuggled closer.

His body reacted immediately and visibly. Apparently, making love twice last night hadn't been enough. He considered seeing if she was willing to…

No, that would be asking too much.

"Sorry I woke you," he said.

"I've been drifting in and out a while now."

He hadn't noticed. "I hope my snoring didn't bother you."

"Only for the first hour." She rolled onto her back, then her side in order to face him. He must have looked dismayed for she laughed and said, "I'm joking. You don't snore."

He kissed her just for the fun of it. She, and not he, took the kiss to another level and melded her body to his. When his phone alarm went off, he reluctantly reached over to the night stand, silenced the alarm and exhaled slowly.

"Don't tell me," she said. "Duty calls."

"I'm overseeing the morning and evening horse feedings while Josh is gone. Can't let him down my first day on the job."

"Coffee?" She threw off the sheet covering them.

"Love some." He openly stared at her shapely backside as she sat up. "Mind if I shower first? I'll be quick."

"Not at all." She turned her head and gave him a saucy smile. "Mind if I shower with you?"

Quinn sprang off his side of the bed. The next instant, he was carrying her into the adjoining master bathroom and shoving open the shower stall door. With one hand, he turned on the faucets.

"Wait!" Summer shrieked and twisted sideways to avoid the spray. "The water's cold."

"I'll make up for it."

Rather than rush, they took their time. The liquid soap smelled flowery but made a thick, rich lather that he rubbed all over her, taking extra care with her round, full breasts and curvy behind. When he slid his fingers between her legs, her soft moans were all the encouragement he needed to continue until she shuddered and went weak in his arms.

"Mmm." She clung to him, her arms circling his neck. "I like."

"Not half as much as I do."

Refusing to be left out, she poured a generous dollop of liquid soap into her palm. Starting with his chest, she worked her way down to his stomach.

Don't stop.

Quinn gulped when her hand closed around his erection, shut his eyes and leaned his head back. "I hope you're serious."

"Very." She stood on tiptoes, alternately licking, kissing and nibbling his neck and shoulder.

He tried. Really he did. When he could stand it no more, he hooked an arm behind her left knee and lifted her leg, then entered her deliberately and powerfully. She gasped and clutched him, uttering something wicked that instantly propelled Quinn to the edge. Toppling over was simply a matter of letting go.

"You're incredible," he murmured, holding her tight. Hot water ran down their sides, washing away the soap.

"You inspire me to be incredible."

They finished with the shower and toweled each other off. Though spent, Quinn was unable to keep his hands or mouth off Summer, leaving her no choice but to scurry out of the bathroom.

A moment later, she reappeared wearing a robe. "I'll put some coffee in a travel mug. You can return it later."

"Tonight?"

Her smile faded the tiniest amount. "Let's see."

He nodded, silently scolding himself for pushing. "I'll be right there."

Dressed, he joined her in the kitchen and accepted the

travel mug she held out to him. The hot brew tasted good going down.

"I borrowed your toothbrush. Hope you don't mind."

"What if I do?"

"It's a little late, I guess."

She laughed again. "You're an easy target."

"Maybe I like you teasing me."

They sat at the breakfast bar and talked about nothing in particular. Unfortunately, he couldn't linger. Not if he wanted to be done with the morning horse feeding and his other chores before Jenny arrived with Corrine.

Summer sipped her coffee. "Depending on what time Hal gets here and what mood Teddy's in, I should be at the ranch before ten."

"We may still be at the Cowboy Up Café. I'm taking Corrine and Jenny to breakfast."

"Good!" Summer seemed genuinely pleased. "We'll catch up afterward, and you can tell me how it went, which I'm sure will be wonderful."

Her comment reminded him of Marty's suggestion to initiate a discussion with Jenny regarding visitation. Wonderful might not happen.

"I hope so. As long as I take her riding, Corrine will be happy. Not calling me Dad yet."

"Give her time."

"I want Jenny to let me tell her I'm her father."

"Corrine's very young. Be patient. That's a lot to comprehend for someone who hasn't had a father before."

The front doorbell rang, interrupting Quinn's response. They exchanged glances, and he checked the time on the oven clock. It was barely seven.

"Are you expecting anyone?"

"No." Summer frowned, straightened her robe and retied the belt.

Quinn grabbed his cowboy hat off the counter and followed her into the living room, just in case her visitor was an unwelcome one. They'd yet to reach the door when a familiar shrieking started on the other side.

"Teddy!" Summer hurried the last few feet, disengaged the dead bolt and yanked open the door.

Hal stood there, holding a leash attached to a spaniel dog who yipped and wagged its tail excitedly. Teddy emerged from behind Hal. Both wore frustrated expressions.

Hal's turned to anger when he spotted Quinn. "What's he doing here?"

Summer ignored him and extended an arm to Teddy. "Sweetie, what's wrong?"

Teddy ran past Hal, then, as if noticing Quinn for the first time, came to an abrupt halt in front of him.

"Man." He stood there, shaking from head to toe, his gaze focused on the floor.

"Hi, son."

"He's not your son," Hal bit out between clenched teeth.

Teddy inched closer to Quinn and grabbed one of his belt loops. He swore he heard the boy's soft sob.

"Get away from him." Hal stepped over the threshold, jabbing the air with his index finger. "You hear me?"

The dog strained against the leash. Hal let go, and the dog bounded past them to the kitchen, toenails rapidly clicking on the tile floor.

"Stupid mutt."

Teddy glowered at his father and made a hissing sound.

Summer positioned herself in front of Hal. "Leave him alone."

Who was she referring to? Teddy, Quinn or Paw Paw?

Hal glared at her. "I told you to keep him away from Teddy."

"It's seven in the morning. Did you actually pick up Teddy at this hour? And why bring him home? Oh, wait. Don't tell me. He acted up and you couldn't handle him."

"I don't want our son exposed to your tawdry—"

"Nothing I'm doing or did is tawdry, and he wouldn't be exposed to anything if you could—" she lowered her voice "—tolerate being with him for more than ten whole minutes."

Teddy hissed again and tugged harder on Quinn's belt loop.

Quinn hated leaving but he was undoubtedly adding to Summer's troubles. Donning his hat, he nodded at her and started for the door. "I'll call you."

"No!"

The objection came from Teddy and surprised not only Quinn, but his parents, too, judging by their expressions.

He put a hand on Teddy's back. "I have to go, son. My daughter's coming to the ranch. But I'll see you there later, okay?"

Teddy slowly nodded and let go of Quinn's belt loop.

Wasn't that something? Teddy had understood Quinn. It was the first time he'd truly communicated with the boy. Too bad it was under these circumstances.

"Goodbye," he told Summer, regretting that he couldn't hug and kiss her. Hal was already angry enough. Any show of affection would send him through the roof.

"I'm not joking." It seemed as if Hal wasn't ready to let Quinn leave. "You stay away from my son, or I'll get a restraining order."

It was a hollow threat, but Quinn didn't call the man on it. He was reacting out of anger, and perhaps jealousy. Quinn knew the feeling.

"I'm so sorry," Summer said, regret tinging her voice.

Quinn ignored the furious glare Hal aimed at him and

addressed Summer. "Don't worry about it. None of this is your fault."

"Very sweet." Hal's tone dripped sarcasm. "Now get out."

Quinn's fist itched to connect with the man's jaw and, for a moment, he let himself picture just that. Better sense prevailed. Hal was exactly the kind of guy to press charges. Quinn wouldn't give him the satisfaction.

"This is my house." Summer faced Hal with a fearlessness Quinn admired. "I say who stays and who goes. And you're the one who's going first."

Hal drew himself up. "I'll see you on Wednesday. Have Teddy ready on time for a change, will you?"

"Keeping him for another ten whole minutes?" she called after him before shutting the door and falling against it. She gave Quinn a disarming look. "Wow, that was pretty immature of me."

He grinned. "You're entitled."

Teddy made a sound Quinn hadn't heard before and, spinning on his heels, called for Paw Paw as he ran toward the kitchen. He thought the boy might be crying and need his animal companion. Understandable since he'd just witnessed his parents arguing.

"Oh, my gosh." Summer beamed and grabbed Quinn by the arm, shaking it soundly. "He's laughing. I haven't heard that in years."

Her joy gave Quinn hope that, with a little luck, they might actually have a shot at a future. Hadn't his own recent release shown him anything was possible?

"THIS PLACE IS GREAT." Jenny beamed at Quinn from across their booth. "Really quaint. And kid-friendly." She looked around at the many filled tables on this Sunday morning, most of them filled with families.

"I like it."

The Cowboy Up Café had become one of his favorite places in Mustang Valley. "The atmosphere's good and the food's better." To emphasize his point, he took a bite of his scrambled eggs.

"Me, too!" Corrine sat beside him, elevated by a child's booster seat, her purple pony tucked between them. She stabbed her waffle with her fork and brought a large, syrup-coated piece to her mouth. Half the syrup wound up on her face. Not caring, she chewed enthusiastically, her cheeks chubby like a chipmunk's.

Quinn looked down at her expressive brown eyes and fell a little bit more in love. How was he going to say goodbye to her in a few hours?

Not for the first time this weekend, he contemplated all the recent good in his life. His family, his freedom, his job, Summer and Teddy, and this sweet little girl sitting next to him.

"Wipe your face, baby." Jenny handed Corrine a paper napkin.

The girl halfheartedly dabbed at the syrup, then quickly lost interest in favor of her orange juice, which she slurped loudly.

Quinn copied her, and Corrine giggled. "You're funny."

She might have called him Daddy for all the warm feelings stirring inside him. This must be what it was like to be a parent.

He understood better than ever Summer's devotion to Teddy. Like her, Quinn would go to the ends of the earth to protect and cherish his child and ensure a future with her. Jenny had been accommodating this weekend, but things could change. She might return home, think about losing her daughter several times a year, potentially for weeks at a time, and decide to go into hiding again.

Quinn noticed her checking her watch. They'd have to leave soon in order to make their flight. Jenny mentioned she hoped Corrine would nap most of the trip, something more likely to occur on a full stomach.

"Thank you for brunch," Jenny said.

"My pleasure."

"Are we keeping you from helping with the reception cleanup?"

"There'll be plenty of people there."

"Including Summer?"

"Possibly." Quinn strived to maintain a neutral tone.

He'd arrived late at the ranch after leaving Summer's this morning. After making sure the horses were fed, he'd then headed to the apartment for a shave and change of clothes. He'd finished just as Jenny called to let him know she and Corrine were pulling into the driveway.

To his delight, Corrine had greeted him happily, even running the last few feet. He'd taken her on a short ride, naturally. Quinn had begun to worry that horses were all Corrine would ever want from him, so he'd suggested she might like the swing set and sandbox in the backyard of the ranch house.

When Quinn had sat in the sandbox with Corrine and helped her dig a hole, she'd been thrilled, and some of the barriers between them fell away. He would remember that moment always. When they'd arrived at the café a half hour ago, she'd insisted on sitting next to him. He'd remember that, too.

The only downside had been when she asked his name, something he and Jenny had tactfully avoided these past two days. Quinn would have told her then and there that she was his daughter, but Jenny's warning glance had stopped him.

In the end, he'd simply said "Quinn," which Corrine had repeated several times.

"Look." She lifted her straw out of her orange juice and blew it at Quinn, spraying him with droplets.

"That's enough, Corrine," Jenny scolded.

"It's all right." Quinn didn't mind and even chuckled.

"She shouldn't be allowed to get away with bad behavior."

"Okay."

Would Corrine be spitting orange juice droplets on people when she was twenty? Hardly. He winked at her when Jenny's head was turned. Corrine melted his heart by trying to wink back at him and only succeeding in squinting both eyes.

"You think I'm overreacting," Jenny said, tension creeping into her voice.

"I don't. But I should warn you, I'll overindulge her at first and maybe for a while. I can't help it."

"Fine." Her lips thinned.

"It was just some orange juice."

"Let's not argue, Quinn."

"Quinn!" Corrine echoed and grinned up at him.

"That's right." He touched his index finger to the tip of her nose and earned a giggle for his efforts. After a moment, when she was again distracted, he asked Jenny, "When do you think I might be able to see her next?"

Marty had wanted him to test the waters about visitation. Probably not the best time to bring it up, except Jenny and Corrine were leaving soon.

"About that—"

"I want eggs," Corrine suddenly demanded.

"Sure." Quinn started to signal the waitress.

"She can have eggs when she finishes her waffle,"

Jenny said with a firmness that let him know the topic wasn't open for debate.

"Want eggs," Corrine insisted, her mouth pursed in a stubborn frown.

Quinn thought he saw in his daughter a bit of the same temper he struggled with on a daily basis. She would have to inherit that quality from him, too.

"You finish your waffle—" he tugged on one of her brown curls "—and I'll give you a piggyback ride to the truck."

"Yay!" Corrine threw her arms up into the air, her fork slipping from her fingers and landing with a clatter on the table.

"Corrine!" Jenny admonished. "Settle down."

Quinn bit his tongue. He refused to ruin this last hour with his daughter by fighting with Jenny.

An elderly couple passed their table on their way out. The woman gave the three of them a fond smile and a friendly hello. "What a beautiful child."

"We're very lucky," Jenny answered.

The couple continued on, the woman obviously mistaking them for a family. It was an easy enough assumption to make, and Quinn supposed they were a family, if a little unusual.

He shifted uncomfortably. Thinking of him, Corrine and Jenny together made him feel disloyal to Summer. When he was with her and Teddy, he also felt as if *they* were a family.

"About my next visit with Corrine," he started.

Jenny sipped her coffee. "I was thinking we could begin slowly."

"How slow?" Quinn cautioned himself to remain calm and not get upset before there was a valid reason.

"Here, baby." Jenny pushed the crayons and printed

sheet the waitress had left at Corrine and waited for her to start coloring. "What if I bring her to California in a couple months to meet your parents?"

He sat back. "My parents?"

"Don't they want to meet her?"

"Um, very much. More than you can imagine. I just…"

"Didn't think I'd cooperate?" She raised her brows.

"Please don't jump to conclusions. I really had no idea what to expect."

"I'm not," she assured him. "I've actually thought a lot about this. To be honest, this weekend has gone better than I anticipated. And Corrine has really taken to you."

He grinned at his busily scribbling daughter. "It's mutual."

"I always did like your parents and, as it turns out, I'm taking a week off work in mid-October. In part to use up some extra vacation days before the end of the year and to celebrate Corrine's birthday. If you and your parents are willing, Corrine and I could meet you in Bishop. We can drive there in one day."

"One long day."

The trip had to be at least fifteen or sixteen hours and was eighteen or more hours for him. Then again, Bishop was a sensible halfway point.

"Would you mind if Andy came with us?" Jenny asked. "He's already scheduled the time off."

Ah. The boyfriend. How close were he and Corrine? What did she call him?

Quinn didn't like the idea of his daughter spending all day on a road trip with *Andy*. But if he raised objections and Jenny retaliated by withdrawing her offer, then his parents would miss the opportunity to meet their granddaughter. He couldn't let that happen.

"Can Corrine stay a couple nights with my folks?"

"Without me?"

"Yes." He nodded. "I'll be there, of course."

Jenny considered for a moment. "Okay. Your parents are trustworthy."

"And I'm not?"

"That isn't what I meant."

He thought it was, despite her protests. "What about you and Andy? Where will you two stay?"

"In a hotel."

It was Quinn's turn to consider. "I'd like to tell Corrine that I'm her—"

"Don't say it," Jenny hissed.

"It's important to me that she knows."

"More than a visit with your parents?"

Quinn gazed at Corrine, who was coloring outside the lines. She seemed to have lost interest in having eggs or even finishing her waffle.

"You're going to make me choose?" he asked.

"She's too young to understand."

"Maybe at first. She will eventually."

Jenny stared out the window beside them for a full minute before saying, "What if we compromise? You give me the next two months to prepare Corrine and then we tell her together during the visit to your parents."

He nodded. "I can live with that."

"By then, perhaps, we'll have reached an agreement."

"I should also know more on my suit against the state."

"Are you still willing to relocate?"

Quinn hesitated. Prior to last night, he'd have answered yes. Now Summer factored into any decision he made, even though they hadn't yet defined their relationship.

"For the time being, I'm staying here. At least until my legal struggles are resolved."

"What about Summer?"

Was he that transparent?

Quinn's instincts continued to tell him the less said about Summer the better. "We're just friends."

"Come on." Jenny studied him from her side of the booth. "I saw the way you looked at her. You used to look at me like that."

"I'm not in a position to date. I have a lot on my plate."

"You're really going to play dumb?" She might have said more, but her phone suddenly beeped from its place beside her plate. She picked up the phone and read the text message, then muttered a sound of distress.

"What is it?" Quinn asked.

"A message alert. Our flight's been delayed." She read more, then groaned. "That's what I get for flying one of those discount airlines." She groaned again. "Excuse me. I need to call them."

Quinn took the opportunity while Jenny was occupied to play with Corrine. He made her a swan out of a dollar bill, similar to the one he'd made for his niece and nephew at the welcome party his cousins had given him. She was completely enthralled with the swan and named it Gertie. The purple pony had been dubbed Lilac.

"Well, this sucks." Jenny pressed her fingers to her forehead. "We either take our chances and hang out at the airport, or they book us on a later flight that doesn't go out until nine tonight. Nine!" she repeated with obvious irritation.

"Can you get a refund and take a different airline?"

"I used credit card miles. No flexibility." She closed her eyes and breathed deeply. "Corrine isn't used to staying up that late. I don't want her crying the whole flight. The other passengers will hate us."

"You could always stay another day," Quinn suggested.

"I have to get back to work."

"Your employer won't understand?"

"We have a big sales meeting, and I promised my boss I'd be there." She shrugged. "I told the airlines to book us on the nine o'clock flight. But I'm not hanging around the airport for hours with a small child."

"Will you go back to your parents'?"

"I would, except they weren't expecting us to still be here and are going to a friend's pool party. I suppose I could call them."

Quinn tried to contain his excitement. "We could always pass the time at the ranch. There's plenty to do."

"Corrine will need a nap."

"She can sleep in my apartment. On the couch," he said when Jenny gave him a look.

She wavered.

Honestly, Quinn expected her to decline and insist on spending more time with her parents. Instead, she both threw him for a loop and made his day by answering, "All right."

Chapter Ten

Quinn stared at the sky. According to Summer, cloud cover in August wasn't rare. The temperature dropping to the midnineties? Now that, apparently, was something to celebrate. As a result, activity at the ranch was greater than usual for a Sunday afternoon.

Along with several of the hands having an informal calf roping contest, led by Quinn's cousin Cole, friends were finishing the reception cleanup and therapy program students visited the horses. They weren't allowed to ride—only during scheduled lessons—but they did pet and play with the horses and give them treats such as carrots and apples. Cara approved, encouraging any interaction that benefitted the students as long as there was a responsible adult to supervise.

At the moment, Quinn was working with the buckskin mare he'd taken from the mustang sanctuary. Jenny and Corrine had gone up to the apartment a while ago and were attempting to rest. It had taken a walk in the community park across from the café and playing with Nathan and Kimberly on the swing set for an hour to finally tire Corrine out.

Quinn had at first worried that his apartment wouldn't meet Jenny's meticulous standards. He remembered her as being fussy when they'd dated. Rather, she declared it cute and had settled with Corrine on the couch, rubbing her back and singing her a song. Quinn had quietly left after showing Jenny how to operate the TV remote.

"Easy, girl," he said to the mare as he ran his hand down her leg, squeezing the long tendon in an attempt to coax her into lifting her foot.

They stood in the shade of the horse stables where Quinn had momentarily stopped. He'd strapped a saddle pad to her back, step one in breaking her to ride. She didn't seem to mind the saddle pad, which was encouraging. They still had a long way to go, and Quinn was glad he'd be around to see the training through.

Sooner or later, he should give the buckskin a name but, so far, he'd drawn a blank. She deserved something more original than Fancy or Lady.

Feeling his phone vibrate before he heard the ring, he straightened. The number on the display wasn't a familiar one, and he almost let the call go to voice mail.

"Hello."

"Quinn Crenshaw?"

"Yes." He started walking the mare again, more to vent his nervous energy than because she needed the exercise. For some reason, the call put him on edge.

"This is Morgan Tedrowe, assistant warden of the prison in Florence."

Now Quinn knew the source of his unease. Must have been his instincts kicking in. No call from a prison warden could be good.

"What can I do for you?" he asked.

"Sorry to call on a Sunday afternoon. I won't be in the office tomorrow, and this can't wait."

Not exactly an answer to his question. Quinn's grip on the lead rope tightened until the rough, scratchy rope cut into his palm.

"Your number was given to me by Warden Harrison." He referenced the senior warden at the prison in California where Quinn had been serving his sentence before his release. "For several months now I've been looking for a former inmate with specific qualifications, and he responded to my query, recommending you. After reviewing your history, I tend to agree with his assessment."

"I'm sorry, sir. I don't understand. Does this have to do with my—" Quinn started to say *exoneration and suit against the state* only to stop himself. Better not tip his hand by revealing too much.

"I apologize. I should have told you from the start." He cleared his throat. "We're expanding our inmate work release program, a goal of mine this past year. Would you be available Wednesday or Thursday to meet and talk?"

"Meet? Why?" Quinn was through beating around the bush, and his abrupt manner no doubt reflected as much. "What does any of this have to do with me?"

"A possible partnership. Allow me to explain," Tedrowe continued when Quinn said nothing. "We already work with a cattle ranch in the Apache Junction area. In exchange for free labor, the ranch provides thoroughly vetted and low-security-risk inmates the opportunity to shave time off their sentences, learn new job skills and reintegrate to civilian life. I won't lie—it also relieves some of the burden on the prison system by reducing costs and freeing up space."

"I'm still confused."

"Perhaps you've heard of similar programs," Tedrowe congenially suggested. "Besides the Apache Junction ranch, we have two Hotshot firefighting teams with the Forest Service."

"Heard of them, yes. But I personally didn't participate in any programs. What reason would you and I have to meet?"

"We—I—happen to think Dos Estrellas would be an excellent ranch where we could start a second program."

"Isn't Mustang Valley far from Florence?"

"An hour each way."

"Look, I'm just an employee here," Quinn insisted. "I have no say in the operations."

"Aren't two of the owners your cousins?" Tedrowe had obviously done his homework. "You could talk to them on our behalf."

"Not about this."

"May I ask what your reservations are?"

"I don't think my family will want inmate laborers at the ranch." Quinn was thinking not only his niece and nephew but students, as well. Their parents were already uneasy about him, and he was innocent. The prisoners in Tedrowe's program weren't. "The ranch has an equine therapy program for special-needs children."

"We're aware of that and can assure you the prisoners would never be there during the sessions."

"It's a lot of responsibility," Quinn said.

"The state would provide liability insurance."

"Too many things could go wrong."

"Which is why I'd like to meet with you and your cousins. Explain all the details. This is a worthwhile program. You must see that."

"I'm sure of it."

Tedrowe didn't discourage easily. "The only way this program can succeed is by having an individual in place acting as liaison between the ranch and the prisoners. We'd like you to be that individual. Because of your history, the prisoners will respect you and you'll relate to them in a way even the most seasoned and trained professional can't."

"Sir—"

"The position comes with a salary." He cited an amount. "It's negotiable."

Quinn pulled up short, the buckskin bumping into him. For someone else, the amount wasn't outrageously high. For Quinn, it represented more than he could possibly expect to earn, at least until his record was cleared.

Did Tedrowe know Quinn was fighting for shared custody of his daughter and using money as incentive to win him over? Maybe. Maybe not. Jobs were hard to come by for ex-cons. He might be counting on that reality to sway Quinn.

"I have to think about it."

Tedrowe continued to pressure Quinn. "Can we set up the meeting for Thursday afternoon? Say, two o'clock? You or your cousins can call me before then with any questions."

"How about I think on this for a while and call you?"

Quinn might bounce the proposition off Josh and get his cousin's feedback, especially where Cara and the students were concerned. He doubted she'd agree. On the other hand, there was all that free labor. For a ranch that had recently recovered from near financial disaster, the proposal was worth considering.

"Fine," Tedrowe conceded.

Quinn could tell the assistant warden had really wanted to set that appointment and was disappointed he hadn't. After discussing a few more details, and Tedrowe making one last bid for a Thursday appointment, they disconnected. Quinn pocketed his phone and headed to the row of outdoor stalls behind the stables.

The buckskin's stall happened to be next to those of

the therapy program horses. Two families were there with their kids, along with Summer and Teddy. Quinn had been hoping to run into her, and his heart soared.

She and Teddy were facing away from him and intent on petting Stargazer. She probably assumed he was with Corrine and Jenny, driving them to the airport. That gave Quinn a chance to study Summer without her being aware of it, and he took full advantage, quickly putting the buckskin away and then leaning against the top railing.

She'd changed into a green dress with skinny straps holding it up. Not that the dress was immodest—she took care in how she dressed around Teddy—but it showed enough leg below the hem and enough bare shoulders to fuel Quinn's every fantasy. He'd thoroughly enjoyed running his palm along her shoulders last night in bed and entwining his legs with her trim, shapely ones beneath the sheet covering them.

"Hi, Quinn." The greeting came from Lizzie, the little girl with Down syndrome, and roused Quinn from his reverie.

He spun. "What's shaking, kid?"

"Not much."

Lizzie was alone, having apparently escaped her mother's watchful eye. She was a lot like his nephew in that regard.

"Where's your mom?" he asked, glancing about.

"In the bathroom. I'm supposed to be waiting right there." She indicated a spot thirty feet down the row of stalls. "And not moving an inch."

"But you did."

She made a face. "I said hi to you, but you didn't hear me. What was I supposed to do?"

Before Quinn could answer, Lizzie's mother came running out from the horse stables where the restroom was located. She appeared shaken, as if she'd encountered a nest of black widow spiders beneath the sink.

"Lizzie!" she called. "Get over here."

"I'm just saying hi to Quinn."

"Afternoon, ma'am." He tugged on the brim of his cowboy hat. "Lizzie is—"

"Let's go, young lady. Right now." The woman didn't give her daughter a chance to respond and practically hauled her away.

Okay, maybe *hauled* was too strong of a description, but she'd done her best to quickly remove Lizzie from Quinn's vicinity and hadn't spared him a single glance. It was weird, he decided, and he might have spent more time dwelling on it if Summer hadn't finally noticed him. Wasting no time, he sauntered over to her and Teddy.

She smiled like a woman glad to see her man. Quinn figured he must be wearing a pretty dopey grin himself. His cheeks actually hurt.

"You came," he said.

"We're visiting Stargazer." She nodded at Teddy, who was petting the placid horse though the stall rails.

The boy turned his head and, as had happened before, made direct eye contact with Quinn.

"Be careful that horse doesn't bite you." He was joking, of course.

Teddy seemed to understand and made the same garbled noise he had before. Laughter. It was the second time today Quinn had seen Teddy display a sense of humor.

"Corrine and Jenny get off all right?" Summer asked.

Quinn explained about the cancelled flight, Jenny booking a later one and the nap in his apartment. "We're leaving for the airport about six."

Summer's gaze traveled to Teddy. "We have a lesson in a short while."

"Today? It's Sunday."

"The program director sent out an email. Because the weather's cooler, they decided to offer an extra lesson on a first come, first serve basis."

"That's great." Quinn moved marginally closer to Summer. Enough that he could catch the delicate scent of her lotion. Not so close that they'd draw attention.

"We'll see." Her reply lacked enthusiasm.

"What's wrong?"

She inclined her head, indicating she didn't want Teddy to hear them. Quinn leaned in to hear better.

"Hal insists on coming to the lesson," Summer whispered.

"How did he find out?"

"He's on the email loop. Normally, I wouldn't care, but Teddy's been agitated all day, ever since our little scene this morning. I jumped on the chance for a lesson when the email came. Riding always calms him down. Now I'm afraid just the opposite will happen, and he'll have a meltdown when he sees Hal." She groaned. "Why does he have to come? He doesn't care."

"Because he knows I work here?"

"Would it be selfish of me to say I really hope the adoption agency finds them a baby soon?" She pressed a hand to her face. "That was a terrible thing to say."

"Look, Teddy loves it here. Maybe everything will be all right." Quinn couldn't help himself and touched her arm, keeping the caress brief. "You worrying will only agitate him. He's very perceptive."

"You're right." She touched him back. "Thanks."

Quinn had an idea. "When's the lesson?"

"Four."

"Since we both have some time, why don't we put a halter on Stargazer and let Teddy walk her around the grounds? That way, Stargazer can work her magic on him, and he'll be ready for the lesson."

Summer hesitated. "Okay, but only if you come with us."

"And if Hal sees us?"

Summer shook her head. "I don't care."

"I do," Quinn insisted.

"Well, we're not going without you," she said.

In the end, he relented. Her pleading eyes were too hard to resist. He'd just have to make sure they were done long before Hal arrived. "All right. You win."

Her smile was triumphant. "Come on, sweetie," she called to Teddy. "We're going to take Stargazer for a walk. You, me and Quinn."

"TELL ME EVERYTHING about your brunch with Corrine and Jenny. Did you get a chance to discuss visitation?"

Summer, Quinn and Teddy had been doing their usual, circling the stables with Stargazer in tow. Teddy led the horse several paces ahead of Summer and Quinn. If asked, she'd say she was in a better position to watch Teddy. It was also true she liked walking beside Quinn, their conversation of no interest to Teddy.

During the last two circuits, more vehicles had pulled into the parking area. Soon, students and instructors would be saddling up their horses for the lesson.

"It went great." Quinn's grin was contagious. "You won't believe this. Jenny offered to bring Corrine to my parents' in Bishop."

"You're kidding!"

"For a whole week. In October. I'm driving there to meet them."

This was the best outcome possible. "Have you told your parents yet? They must be ecstatic."

"I was planning on calling them tonight."

Summer couldn't contain the happiness bubbling up inside her. Was it true? Did she and Quinn have a chance at that future she'd thought beyond their reach?

"Jenny could always back out," he cautioned.

"She won't. Why would she?"

"She can be impulsive. One minute, she's generous. The next, she's thinking only of herself."

Summer understood Quinn's reluctance. He'd been disappointed by Jenny before. Summer's job as his friend was to remain positive.

"I can't believe she'd let your parents down. No one's that cruel."

He shrugged, possibly recalling Jenny's disappearance after his conviction.

When they reached the entrance to the stables, he suggested they saddle Stargazer in preparation for the lesson. Summer agreed. She didn't want to hold up the other students more than necessary.

Teddy remained glued to Quinn's side, watching his every move. It was a vast improvement over the days when he just stood at Stargazer's head, ignoring everyone and everything save the horse.

"We didn't talk support." Quinn showed Teddy how to brush the horse's mane without pulling the hair.

"Better to leave those details to the attorneys."

He paused, his gaze meeting hers. "It's really happening."

"It is."

He pulled her to him, his touch igniting a flurry of delightful tremors. He would have kissed her had she allowed it. She didn't. There'd be time for that later, when they were alone and Hal wasn't due to arrive any moment.

"I suppose we need to figure out what's next." She retreated a step, putting a small but respectable distance between them.

"If by what's next you mean what's next with us, yeah. And I can't wait."

"Not much has changed, Quinn."

"After last night, I'd say a heck of a lot has changed."

"We need to go slow."

"As long as we're moving forward, I can handle slow." She felt the heat from his gaze as it roamed her face. "I'm going to fight for what I have, Summer. It's important to me."

"I will, too. But nothing definite is happening with us until you and Jenny reach an agreement. At least regarding Corrine."

"Nope." He walked away. "No can do."

She went after him, grabbing his arm. "What?"

"I want to see you again. Soon." He lowered his head to hers. "I insist."

She almost melted at the unguarded longing in his dark eyes. "We'll see."

"Yes, we will."

"Maybe you can come by for dinner later this week. But just dinner." She leveled a finger at him. "I realize we can't go back to where we were—it's too late for that. But Teddy's still my first priority and Corrine is yours."

"Want to see her again before she leaves?"

Summer laughed at his abrupt change. "I'd love to. But what about Jenny?"

He gave her a swift peck on the cheek. "I'll bring Corrine over to watch the lesson. I bet Jenny will be okay with that." He might have kissed her again if not for Teddy's exclamation, startling them both.

"Bit! Bit!"

Summer was embarrassed to admit she'd once again

forgotten about her son, Quinn having demanded all her attention.

"Bit?" She looked at him. "Is he talking about the bridle?"

"He must be."

She reveled in yet another milestone. Teddy was learning the names of the riding equipment. Could her day possibly improve? Summer didn't dare voice the question for fear of jinxing herself.

After Stargazer was fully saddled and bridled, Quinn positioned the stepladder beside her so that Teddy could mount. He put his foot on the first step, then hesitated.

"Uh-oh." She'd worried he might regress and refuse to use the ladder. "Sweetie, what's wrong?"

Pivoting abruptly, he reached out and stuck his index finger through Quinn's belt loop. All right, he needed a little extra encouragement. Who didn't now and then?

Teddy surprised Summer by grabbing her wrist, much like he had Quinn's that one day. She froze, afraid to move, afraid to breathe, afraid he'd let go. He seldom touched her and usually only under duress.

"Sweetie," she whispered.

"Maw."

The small tug on her wrist released a flood of emotions. Joy. Relief. Excitement. Even sorrow. Tears pricked her eyes. Teddy wasn't just communicating. He was *connecting*, physically and emotionally, with her *and* Quinn. This was a rare and remarkable moment.

Sadly it didn't last. Teddy let go of both her and Quinn. He skillfully climbed the ladder and plunked down into the saddle as if he'd mounted horses from the day he could walk.

Extending his arms in front of him, he said, "Ride, ride."

Quinn placed the reins in Teddy's hands and faced Summer. "You okay? You look a little funny."

She wiped at her damp cheeks. "I'm fine. Seriously." Who was she kidding? She was over the moon. Best day ever.

"Let's get out of here." Quinn took hold of the lead rope, and the three of them started down the aisle.

"Don't you think it's strange no one else came by the tack room to saddle their horse or use the hitching rail?"

"Are we early?"

She checked her phone. The lesson was scheduled to start in ten minutes. "No."

Could everyone else have saddled up while she, Quinn and Teddy were circling the horse stables? She supposed it was possible.

As they reached the wide entrance, several things became simultaneously apparent, every one of them alarming.

A small gathering of parents had formed thirty feet away, Mindy and the Gonzaleses among them. The sight gave Summer a start, as did Hal and his wife approaching from the parking lot. They headed straight for the small group of people and were readily welcomed, people parting to let them in.

Where were the students? Summer glanced about, her unease growing. They must be at the horse stalls or the arena.

"What's going on?" she murmured, not really expecting Quinn to answer her.

"I have no idea." He stopped and handed Summer the horse's lead rope. "But there's Hal and his wife. I should leave. He doesn't look happy."

"No. Stay." Summer wasn't sure what to do, but retreating didn't feel like the right choice. She had to stand her ground with Hal. Show him he didn't intimidate her.

As Summer and Quinn waited, everyone in the gathering continued to stare, which, frankly, gave Summer the creeps. Lizzie's mom spoke quietly out of the side of her mouth to Hal and his wife. He scowled while his wife covered her mouth in shock.

"Something's not right," Quinn said.

The next instant, Cara emerged from the group. She strode toward them, her steps determined, her posture rigid and her expression grim.

Summer started at the sound of Quinn's phone chiming. He grabbed it and read the text message.

"Corrine's awake from her nap. Jenny's bringing her down."

Teddy, always sensitive to his surroundings, began to hum, and not his this-is-fun tune. The rocking followed. Summer assumed he'd seen Hal and his stepmother at the edge of the group and that was the cause. If not for the many cold stares pinning them in place, she'd have suggested she and Quinn make a run for it.

So much for her perfect day. "I don't like this," she said as Cara neared.

Jenny and Corrine appeared at the bottom of the apartment stairs next to the tack room. Jenny called to Quinn.

"Just a minute," he answered, motioning for her to wait.

The little girl had yet to fully wake and was rubbing her eyes. She brightened at the sight of Quinn. When she would have run toward them, Jenny heeded Quinn's warning and held her back.

At that moment, Cara descended on them. "Quinn, do you have a second? We need to talk. There's a problem."

"Sure." He glanced over his shoulder at Corrine and Jenny. "I just—"

"This is important," Cara said. "And urgent."

"I'm not going anywhere until you tell me what's going on."

Her glance briefly sought out the crowd of people behind her before returning to Quinn. "I'd rather not say here. Is there somewhere private we can go?"

Summer's anxiety skyrocketed, as did Teddy's humming.

She studied the group of parents, especially Mindy. This *had* to do with the petition Mindy had been circulating against Quinn. No other explanation made sense.

"How long will this take?" he asked Cara, shifting impatiently.

"I'm not sure. A little while."

"I have to drive Jenny and Corrine to the airport."

"Please, Quinn."

"We can go to my apartment," he finally relented, "but I'm talking to my daughter first. Don't try to stop me."

He and Cara started out together but not before he sent Summer a backward glance she interpreted as *Wait for me.*

She wished she could go with him and be part of the discussion, but she didn't dare suggest it.

While he stopped to chat with Jenny, Cara continued up the apartment stairs. Summer fidgeted, feeling the stares increase. Did she dare take Teddy to the arena for the lesson and walk past that den of vipers?

"I hungry," Corrine announced in her child's voice.

Summer was close enough to hear most of what Quinn said to Jenny.

"Why don't you take her to the ranch house? The back door is open, and Raquel always leaves snacks out on the counter or in the fridge. I'm pretty sure there's some crackers in the pantry."

Jenny wavered. "We wouldn't be intruding?"

"Not at all. I'll text Raquel and be there shortly. Ten minutes, tops."

Except, Summer didn't think Quinn's discussion with Cara would end that soon.

She'd have offered to go with Jenny and Corrine if not for Teddy's increasing agitation. A quick look around revealed Hal and his wife advancing on them. Summer had no choice but to deal with them or risk Teddy unraveling.

Squaring her shoulders, she gave Quinn one last backward glance, hoping his conversation with Cara wasn't about a demand he be let go from the program and knowing in her heart it was.

Dammit! Why hadn't she warned him or at least spoken to Cara? She'd been distracted by the wedding, not to mention stupidly believing Mindy had come to her senses. Now Quinn was about to be blindsided, and it was all Summer's fault.

Chapter Eleven

"Come in," Quinn said, meeting up with Cara on the apartment landing.

Opening the door, he stepped aside and let her precede him. He didn't mind admitting he was nervous about what lay ahead, though he kept reminding himself there was no reason.

Had she been unhappy with him taking Stargazer out? That must be it. Technically, Teddy was supposed to be supervised by a therapy program staff member when he interacted with the horse. Rules were in place for a reason, and the program was liable if something went wrong.

An image of the parents gathered outside the stables filled his vision. Had they complained to Cara? Did they think Summer and Teddy were receiving special attention or privileges denied their children? It was entirely possible. From what Quinn had witnessed, parents were willing to start a small revolt if they believed their children had been treated unfairly.

No problem. He'd apologize to Cara. Apologize to every parent if necessary. Quinn wasn't above humbling himself when warranted.

"Can I get you a cold drink?" He was already heading for the kitchen.

"No, thanks. I'm good for now."

As he removed a bottled water from the refrigerator, he noticed Cara staring oddly at the couch.

Of course. How could he have forgotten? According to Josh, several years ago Cara had lived in this same apartment with her then young son. After the boy died in an unexpected and tragic fall, she'd moved out. Even though the accident hadn't occurred on the ranch, the memories of her time here with her son had been too painful to endure.

Being in the apartment must be like walking through a portal into her past. Quinn could relate. One of the things he'd done after his release was take a trip to the bar where his personal nightmare had begun. He'd thought the trip might set his demons free.

He'd been wrong. Returning to his hometown and grandparents' place had worked much better. Coming to Dos Estrellas and meeting Summer had banished his demons completely.

All right, not completely. But some days.

Quinn studied Cara, torn between acknowledging her apparent discomfort and ignoring it. Finally he said, "Would you rather go somewhere else?"

"No. This is fine."

She drew herself up, much like she had earlier when she'd come at Quinn and Summer with purpose, and made straight for the small table and chairs in the dining area. "Let's sit here."

It was almost a question, and Quinn wondered if she, too, was nervous. Cara possessed a tender heart and doubtlessly didn't like delivering unpleasant news of any sort.

She sat and waited for him.

Dropping down into the chair across from her, he said, "I don't want to rush you, but I'm worried about Corrine and Jenny. I sent them to the main house for snacks. Corrine was hungry. Problem is, Jenny's not comfortable and feels like they're imposing."

He was also worried about Summer, though he didn't mention her. He had hated leaving her alone with Hal. If Cara weren't his boss when it came to the therapy program and mustang sanctuary, he would blow her off.

"I appreciate your concern," Cara said. "I'll try to be as brief as possible."

He attempted a grin, hoping to put them both at ease. His mouth refused to cooperate. "Sounds serious."

"I'm afraid it is."

"Just tell me," he insisted when she hesitated.

"For the record, I'm speaking to you as the head of the therapy program and your employer, not as your cousin's wife."

"Okay."

"I've, um, received some…complaints about you."

"Yeah, I figured as much."

She drew back in surprise. "You did?"

"Sorry about taking Stargazer out earlier. I know Teddy's supposed to have a program staff member with him at all times. It's wrong and against the rules, and I won't do it again."

Cara cut him off. "That's not the complaint. Or, only a very small part of it."

"What then?"

"Quinn, I'm really, really sorry to have to say this. If I had a choice—if I'd known in advance what was going on—I'd have been able to put a stop to things before they spiraled out of control."

For the second time today, someone was beating around the bush, and Quinn didn't like it. "Just cut to the chase."

She sighed. "Some of the parents have approached me

and expressed their concerns about your involvement with the therapy program and the students."

Idiot. He should have seen this coming, realized it was his past and not Summer or Teddy. That was what he got for having his head in the clouds these past weeks.

"My prison record," he said. "They don't want an ex-con near their kids."

"I'm sorry to admit that's true."

"Except for Teddy, I have almost no contact with the students. Just the horses." He remembered Lizzie, the girl with Down syndrome. "Other than saying hi now and again."

"You have more contact than you realize. But, I agree it's innocuous for the most part."

For the most part? Quinn frowned and struggled to keep his temper in check. "It was bound to happen. I warned you in the beginning not to hire me."

She leaned forward and rested her elbows on the table. "I'm also sorry to say that's not the only complaint, and the other ones are considerably more serious."

"Other ones?"

"There have been two incidents reported involving the children."

"Incidents?" He spoke slowly. "You have to be joking."

"Your actions have come into question."

He shook his head. "I haven't done anything more than talk to the kids. And half the time, it's from the other side of a fence."

"Apparently not."

"You're wrong."

"I hope I am." She spoke with sincerity. "I need you to tell me your version of events."

For a moment, Quinn was thrown back in time to the police station and the tiny interrogation room where he'd been sequestered for hours and hours. The detectives who questioned him hadn't been anywhere near as nice as Cara. They'd repeatedly badgered him, trying to coerce a confession from him.

"What events?" Quinn asked, his jaw barely moving and sweat forming on his brow. He resisted wiping it away, believing he'd look guilty if he did.

"Let's start with the boy you roughed up," Cara said.

He stood so fast his legs hit the table, causing it to wobble precariously. She grabbed the edge with both hands and steadied it.

"I have never touched any kid in the program other than Teddy," he bit out. "And that was only with affection."

"Please calm down, Quinn. Getting upset won't help."

Gritting his teeth, he sat, reminding himself to stay in control and not fly off the handle. This was too important.

"Whoever said that is lying."

"It's one of the students' parents. The student's older brother told them you grabbed him and, according to the parents, manhandled him and tried to take his money."

No, no, no! "That's absurd and not what happened."

"Which is why we're having this discussion."

"The kid was beating up Nathan. Had him pinned down on the ground and was clobbering him. Did he by chance mention that to his parents?"

"If he did, they didn't tell me."

"Of course not." Quinn snorted with derision.

"Anything else?"

"I did pull the kid off Nathan," he admitted. "That's true. And held on to his shoulder until I could get the whole story."

"Did anyone else see what happened?" Cara asked.

"Summer was there. And Teddy."

"Anyone else?"

"What's wrong? Summer's not a reliable enough witness because we're friends?" At Cara's curious look, Quinn wondered if she knew the full extent of their relationship. Summer and Cara *were* close, so it was likely Summer might have told her. "Fine, don't answer," he said before Cara could speak. "Josh will also verify my story. Except, he's my cousin and might be considered biased. Or there's Nathan, if you're willing to take the word of a three-year-old."

"Please, Quinn, don't get angry with me. This isn't personal. I'm head of the therapy program and have a responsibility to thoroughly investigate all complaints. Even the ones that appear far-fetched."

"Are far-fetched." Quinn drew in a long breath, willing his escalating blood pressure to lower. "You know Nathan was hurt. Josh told me you even took care of Nathan that night."

"I did wash him up and put ice on his injuries. But I didn't see what happened. I knew only what Josh told me."

"Why didn't you ask me about the fight the next day?"

"You're absolutely right. I should have. The way Josh told the story, I didn't think it was a big deal. That part is my fault, for sure."

"Will you tell that to the parents?"

"Yes, but they aren't exactly receptive at the moment. Probably because that's not the only complaint. Another parent claims she witnessed you harming a different boy."

"That's ridiculous. Don't tell me they're talking about Teddy."

"Not Teddy. According to the parent, you dragged this boy across the backyard by his leg and refused to release him even when he screamed out in pain."

Quinn ripped off his cowboy hat and threw it across the room to the couch. It missed and hit the floor.

Was he fated for the rest of his life to have people accuse him of terrible deeds he didn't commit?

"That was Nathan."

"Nathan?" Cara's brows rose. "Again?"

"He got a nail stuck in his foot and pitched a fit. It was the day before the wedding. We were helping decorate the backyard. You can ask Summer and Josh about that, too, if you don't believe me. Also Gabe. He was there."

"You weren't dragging Nathan?"

"Hell, no. I did have a hold of his foot. I was trying to get his sneaker off. Didn't Josh tell you?"

"I don't remember. I had a lot on my mind. We were busy." She nodded. "I'll ask him now, though. And Summer and Gabe. Please don't say anything to them until I've had a chance."

"They'll corroborate everything I told you."

"That's good."

"Is there more?" He resented his flippant tone the moment the words were out.

"You have to understand, Quinn. These are grave allegations. I can't dismiss them."

"I'm sick and tired of defending myself when I didn't do anything."

She looked chagrined. "The parents have also given me a petition. They're demanding I terminate your employment."

"They all signed it?"

"About half."

Did Summer know about the petition? If so, why hadn't she told him?

"What do you want me to do?" he asked. "Quit?"

"Nothing yet. Give me some time to sort through this." She paused. "Maybe it would be best if you didn't work with the therapy program horses and avoided taking Teddy out with Stargazer. For a while, anyway."

Her comment hit him with the force of a battering ram. She was treating him as if he were guilty, just like the parents and the police had.

"You're the one who asked me to work with the horses, Cara. You said you trusted me."

"I do trust you."

"Fine."

His cell phone rang, and he glanced at the display. Jenny's number appeared. "Excuse me."

"Go ahead." She stood. "I think we're done for now."

Quinn answered the call. "Hi."

"We're downstairs," Jenny said. "Where are you?"

"On my way." He went over to where his hat had fallen and retrieved it. "Hang tight."

Quinn and Cara left the apartment as they'd entered, with Cara going first. At the bottom of the stairs, Quinn searched for Jenny and Corrine, concerned when he didn't immediately see them.

The group of parents was still gathered at the end of the aisle. If anything, their numbers had increased and now included the program staff members, Josh, and a couple of the ranch hands. Hal, his wife, Summer and Teddy stood off to the side. Hal was talking to Summer and gesturing wildly, whereas her arms were crossed tightly over her middle.

The next moment, Quinn's worst nightmare came true. Jenny emerged from the group of parents, Corrine cradled in her arms. She spotted Quinn and sent him a look filled with question, then accusation.

Dammit to hell.

Quinn charged the group, Cara behind him.

"Quinn, wait," she called.

"I'm through waiting. I didn't do anything wrong."

"Yet."

He slowed his steps, the gravity of the situation sinking in. More than the success of the therapy program and its reputation were at stake. If Quinn was fired, which was looking more and more likely, he'd lose what little income he had and could kiss his request for shared custody goodbye.

Oh, God. What if Jenny believed the parents and their ridiculous accusations? She'd cancel the trip to Bishop and refuse to let him see Corrine again.

The parents could also pull their kids from the program. Without the income the program provided, the ranch would go under again. Josh and Cole might blame Quinn. Ask him to leave the ranch and possibly leave Mustang Valley. That would spell the end of Quinn and Summer's fledgling romance.

Wait. Stop. He was thinking like a guilty man, which he wasn't. He'd told Summer he'd fight for them. Time to prove it.

Lifting his chin and meeting people's stares, he approached the group. He wanted to talk to Summer, but it was Jenny he sought out first.

"What's he doing here?" The demand came from Hal, who strode forward with obvious intentions of confronting Quinn. "The man's a criminal and a child abuser. I don't know about the rest of you, but I'm going to press charges against him."

"Hal, no!" Summer chased after him. "You have this all wrong."

Her protest was too little and too weak to have any impact. The group erupted into a loud, unruly ruckus. Jenny covered Corrine's ears and attempted to shield her with her body.

In that moment, the future Quinn had thought was his for the taking slipped away, gone for good.

SUMMER WATCHED IN horror as Hal incited the parents, first by besmirching Quinn, then verbally attacking him. How could he? She stared, barely recognizing the man she'd once called her husband.

Cara attempted to gain control of the situation but was having little luck. Thankfully, with the exception of Teddy and Corrine, the other children were with the program instructor and staff members, grooming and saddling the horses in preparation for the lesson.

If only Teddy and Corrine were with them. Teddy's agitation continued to increase, his humming growing louder and angrier. Poor Corrine made fearful sounds and clung to her mother.

Why hadn't Jenny left and taken Corrine with her? Summer wouldn't subject Teddy to this scene if she could possibly help it. Unfortunately, in his highly agitated state, she didn't dare touch him, much less physically remove him. Between this morning with Hal and now, Teddy hovered on the brink of a major meltdown.

She glanced over at Quinn, and her heart broke. He stood there, unmoving, angry storm clouds gathering on his face and his hands balled into fists. He hadn't left. Rather, he faced the angry parents, and she admired him more in that moment than ever before.

She also despised Hal. At least, she despised what he was doing, which was using these dire circumstances to advance his own agenda. He'd been furious since this morning when he arrived at her home to find Quinn there, and this was his way of getting even with her.

"Enough," Josh shouted, raising his voice to be heard above the din. "Quinn did nothing wrong. In fact, what he did was behave responsibly. He broke up a fight between my son and an older, bigger boy who was knocking the crap out of him."

"That's not true," the irate mother protested.

Josh spun and stared her down. "Yes, ma'am, it is. My son had the cuts and bruises to prove it."

"He stole my boy's money."

Summer stepped forward. "I was also there, and I saw the whole thing. Nathan did take your son's quarter." She stressed the amount to emphasize how insanely trivial the reason for the fight had been. "But your son could have really hurt Nathan."

"Stealing is wrong."

"So is bullying."

"Nathan took the quarter," Josh said, "and I apologize for his behavior. He's three and still learning right from wrong. That didn't give your son the right to attack him."

"Attack!" She gasped.

"If Quinn hadn't separated the two of them, I'd have been coming after you for assault and battery."

"Don't be ridiculous, they're children," the woman said, clearly affronted.

"My point exactly. I think we should just admit there was wrong on both boys' parts and chalk it up to experience."

The woman lost some of her bravado but didn't back down. "That doesn't excuse *him* for manhandling my son." She glowered at Quinn.

He spoke for the first time. "I merely lifted your son off my nephew, then held on to his shoulder while I tried to sort out what had happened. The next thing I knew, he grabbed the quarter and ran away."

Summer couldn't stand there a moment longer and say nothing. Quinn was omitting a vital part of the story. "Did your son tell you that he kicked Quinn in the shin? Hard enough to raise a welt."

"He was defending himself," the woman said. "What's he supposed to do when an adult grabs him?"

Several people vigorously nodded their heads and murmured agreements.

"He attacked Quinn just like he attacked my son," Josh said.

"You're taking his side simply because he's related to you."

"That's right," Hal concurred. "You're family and will lie for each other."

Summer groaned in frustration and addressed the woman. "We're telling you what we saw. Quinn didn't hurt anyone, regardless of what your son may have told you."

"Are you calling her boy a liar?" Hal accused.

She didn't like this side of him and had thought she'd seen the last of it after their divorce. "I'm saying he didn't relay events exactly as they occurred. If that makes him a liar..."

The woman's cheeks flamed beet red. "Why, you—"

"That's enough," Cara interrupted. She turned pleading eyes on Josh and then Summer. "Please. Let me handle this."

"What about the boy he roughed up?" Hal demanded, not yet ready to give it a rest.

"That's right," Mindy concurred. "Annie saw it, too. We were helping to decorate for the reception."

"That boy," Josh said, "was also my son. And I can assure you he wasn't roughed up by Quinn, on that day or any other one. He stepped on a nail, and Quinn was trying to get it out of his shoe."

Hal confronted Summer. "And I suppose you were there, too. Like you're always with him."

"Don't make this personal, Hal," she answered, but it was too late for that.

"I'm going to take my son out of the program," Mrs. Gonzales said.

"Me, too," another agreed. "Unless you fire him."

The parents were on an unstoppable roll. As if connected by a wire, they craned their necks to stare at Quinn. Was Summer the only one who could see he'd cut off his own arm before hurting a child?

"That isn't necessary," Quinn said, pulling down on the brim of his cowboy hat. "I'll save you the trouble and quit."

"Wait." Cara lifted a hand. "We're going to sort this out. Just give me some time."

"Don't bother."

Summer ached for Quinn. It was obvious he didn't want to be the cause of any trouble for his family and if that included taking the brunt of the responsibility for something he didn't do, then he would.

How did Jenny feel? Did she see the huge sacrifice he was making?

"It's past time for the lesson to start." Cara looked around. "That's what really matters and why we're all here. For our children's sakes. Let's everyone go to the arena. I promise, this will be resolved to your satisfaction, and I'll personally address all of your concerns."

"We want that man gone," Mindy reiterated.

"I said I'd sort this out."

No one moved—except Teddy, who chose that moment to have the mother of all outbursts.

Dropping to the ground, he began rocking back and forth and emitting a strange, high-pitched sound.

"Cripes." Hal groaned and clamped a hand to the side of his head. "Can't you stop him?"

"Sweetie," Summer said softly. "Let's go, okay? Mommy will drive us home."

She wished she had his oversize cowboy hat with them. Maybe she could run to the car and grab it. Or send Hal.

"No, no, no!" Teddy couldn't have spoken clearer.

"All right. We can ride Stargazer if you want."

He flung his arms, pushing Summer away. She inwardly cringed at the grumbles of disapproval from the other parents. They had all of them probably experienced similar public outbursts from their children. Today, however, Summer and Teddy were on display and received no sympathy. Only censure and that was because she'd defended Quinn.

"Can I help?" The offer came from a surprising source. Hal's wife. It was also delivered with kindness, not rancor.

"Thank you. If you could—"

"Man, man, man." Teddy scrambled to his feet, sent Hal a searing glare and barreled straight for Quinn.

"Whoa, there." Quinn held Teddy with both hands and steadied him.

Teddy's finger found Quinn's belt loop. "Staaa."

Summer felt Hal's stare burn into her like the blast from a thousand suns. Jenny's stare, on the other hand, dripped icicles. Summer didn't understand either of them. Quinn had been nothing but good to Teddy.

"Leave my son alone," Hal barked.

"He's not hurting Teddy." Summer stared in confusion. Was everyone blind?

"I told you before—" Hal started for Teddy "—I won't allow a criminal and child abuser near him."

"You're being ridiculous."

"Look, Hal," Quinn said. "I'm only trying to help. Teddy's stressed, and you're adding to it."

The nearer Hal got to Teddy, the more agitated he became. Panic filled his eyes, and his humming intensified until it resembled a swarm of bees. Summer had seen this once before. Teddy had worked himself into such a state of distress, she had feared he'd have a seizure and need to be taken him to the emergency room.

"Stop crowding him." She tried to block Hal. "Give him some space."

"The hell with that." Hal grabbed hold of Teddy's arm. "I'm getting my son out of here."

Hal's touch had the same effect as setting off an explosion. Twisting and screaming, Teddy wrenched free of Hal and threw his arms around Quinn's waist.

"Enough." Hal spoke sharply.

Teddy had never responded well to force, even before he was diagnosed, and dropped to his knees, sobbing and cowering.

"Will someone call the police?"

Summer steeled her resolve. These types of meltdowns were hard to handle when they were alone. In front of an audience, it was excruciating. If she didn't get herself and Teddy out of there this instant, they might be making another trip to the ER.

"Please, Hal," she begged. "Leave him alone."

She must have appeared desperate, for Quinn suddenly picked up Teddy and held him close.

"Easy does it, son. There you go."

Teddy slowly quieted, Quinn's secure embrace working as well as the oversize hat.

"Jenny," Quinn said. "You and Corrine wait for me here. I'm taking Teddy to his mother's car. After that, I'll be right back."

"We'll be in the apartment." Jenny pressed Corrine's head to her chest and walked away.

Summer used to hold Teddy that way when she was

trying to protect him from danger or from something too awful to see.

"You're not taking my son anywhere," Hal barked.

"Yes, I am." Quinn started forward. "You're more than welcome to come with us."

Hal turned to his wife. "Get our attorney on the phone. Now."

She stared at him as if he were a stranger. "No."

"What did you say?"

She spun on her heels and addressed the group. "I think we've all had enough for one day. Let's leave them alone and go about our business."

Good for her, thought Summer. The woman had more backbone than she'd originally given her credit for.

Hurrying after Quinn and Teddy, she caught up to them at her car.

"I'm sorry. What Hal and the other parents said was unforgivable. He's jealous of you and how much Teddy likes you. You must know that. Did you see his wife? She really put him in his place."

"Let's get Teddy settled so you can take him home." Quinn opened the car door and sat Teddy in his booster seat. Finding the hat, he plunked it on Teddy's head.

Summer didn't waste any energy wishing Hal exhibited half the care and affection with Teddy that Quinn did.

"Will you come over tonight?"

"I'm not sure." Quinn's tone worried her.

"We should talk about what happened. Cara isn't going to fire you even if the parents stage a protest."

"I have to get back to Corrine and Jenny." He buckled Teddy's seat belt.

"Yes, of course, but—"

"Not now, Summer."

"I should have done more when Mindy approached me."

Quinn stopped, his hand on the rear passenger door. Teddy still clung to a belt loop. "Yes, you should have."

Summer would have approached if not for fear of agitating Teddy. "I, ah… When Mindy mentioned the petition, I honestly didn't think she'd go through with it. She seemed undecided."

"Why didn't you tell me? You could have prevented a lot of trouble. Those parents are out for blood."

"The whole thing was absurd." Summer blinked back tears. "I didn't want to worry you, not with the wedding looming and with Corrine and Jenny coming for a visit. When nothing came of it, I forgot."

He was right to blame her. What had she been thinking?

"Come over tonight. Please."

"I'll call you."

Was that a polite way of saying no?

Summer felt empty inside and debated about what to do next. This wasn't how their day was supposed to end. Quinn should have taken his daughter and Jenny to the airport, had a cheery goodbye and then come over to Summer's where they'd talk, cuddle on the couch and get to know each other better.

"Tell me everything's going to be all right."

He pulled her into a hug, but it lacked warmth.

"Kiss me."

He did, briefly, his gaze on the horse stables. He didn't need to tell her he was thinking of Corrine and Jenny in the apartment.

His distraction was understandable. She should be supportive and not needy.

"See you later?" She studied his expression.

"Yeah."

Time. That was what he needed. The chance to calm down and put the past hour in perspective.

She drove off, unable to get the scene with the parents out of her mind. Surely Cara would see reason and do the right thing—that being keeping Quinn on the program staff.

"Man, man," Teddy said mournfully from the backseat, his voice muffled by the cowboy hat.

"Yes, man," Summer repeated.

If Quinn didn't call her, she'd call him. Perhaps drop off Teddy at the sitter's and go over to Quinn's.

With a plan in place, she expected to feel a sense of relief. It was slow coming.

Chapter Twelve

The security lines at the airport weren't bad, probably because it was Sunday night rather than Monday morning. Quinn stood with Jenny and Corrine at the entrance to the checkpoint. Their flight wasn't due to leave for another ninety minutes. It wouldn't take them long to clear the security line, especially as Jenny had used express check-in and had only carry-on luggage.

"Don't leave yet." Quinn had been carrying her luggage and didn't let go when she reached for the handle.

Jenny stiffened and withdrew her hand. "I told you on the way here, we have nothing more to discuss."

They'd discussed very little, in fact. She'd cut him short every time he started to speak.

"It isn't what you think," he said. "Cara explained—"

"Save it. My attorney will be in touch."

"Really, Jenny?"

"You'd better get used to it," she scoffed.

She was making this much harder than it had to be. Quinn thought the boyfriend, Andy, might be responsible. All the talking Jenny had done was mostly on the phone with him.

"You haven't changed one bit, Quinn," she continued. "You still have a temper that you can't control."

"I haven't lost my temper in years. No more than most people."

"How can I trust you with Corrine?"

He stared down at his daughter and her pretty cherub face. She'd tucked the purple pony beneath her arm and wore a pink-and-turquoise backpack. This was completely the wrong time to let loose and rage, proving to Jenny she was right. Instead, he bit down hard, cementing his teeth together.

"You can trust me with her," he said evenly as he reached down to stroke Corrine's hair.

The little girl beamed up at him and, for a moment, he tried to imagine everything working out, the two of them riding Hurry Up in the arena and eating at the café with Summer and Teddy. The picture promptly evaporated when Jenny spoke.

"I was wrong to come here." She compressed her mouth into a thin, stern line.

Quinn remembered her doing this before. It had always annoyed him because it signaled her refusal to listen. That had been one of their downfalls. Jenny didn't always have to be right, she just wasn't ever wrong.

"Coming here was absolutely the right thing to do."

She stiffened. "I'm so sorry I had to subject Corrine to that scene earlier."

"No more sorry than I am." She had no idea.

Jenny grabbed hold of Corrine's hand. Tight, as if afraid Quinn would snatch the little girl away. "I shouldn't have to protect my child from an angry mob when she's at her father's."

"*Our* child. And she was never in any danger."

"I've heard this before from you."

"You can't possibly be referring to the night in the bar.

It's been proven beyond a doubt I had nothing to do with that assault."

"But you wanted to hurt that guy when he flirted with me. How do I know you didn't want to hurt the boy, too?"

"You're upset, and you're talking irrationally." Their conversation reminded Quinn of the one they'd had immediately following his release on bail. Jenny had shut down then, too.

"I'm going to have my attorney investigate."

"Great. I welcome an investigator getting to the bottom of this. Make sure he calls the boy's school. I'd bet money he's beaten up other kids besides Nathan."

"You're actually going to pin this on a child?"

Quinn couldn't help himself and raised his voice. "That *child* is a bully. I may have been in a few fights during my lifetime, but I never picked on someone half my size and half my strength."

"Which I suppose makes fighting okay in your opinion." She gaped at him as if he'd spontaneously sprouted devil horns. "You can't see Corrine again."

He counted to ten. Eleven. Twelve. "I will see her. Soon. At my parents' in October."

"You think I'll… I'll…" She sputtered, unable to continue until she collected herself. "I'll take Corrine away again. You won't find us."

Corrine must have sensed the discord between her parents for she began to whimper. "Mommy. I wanna go home."

"Shh. It's all right." Quinn reached for her again.

She immediately quieted and took his hand, holding it between her two tiny ones. Quinn felt every drop of anger drain from him.

Unfortunately, their tender exchange set Jenny off, and she grabbed Corrine. "Leave her alone."

People were starting to stare at them. Quinn decided to back off. He couldn't resist one last warning, however.

"Don't go into hiding again—you could be accused of kidnapping. I have rights, and I won't hesitate to take legal action." All right, he wasn't entirely sure of the kidnapping thing but was glad to see Jenny flustered. "We can work this out. I want that more than anything."

"Is that why you threatened me?"

He almost said she'd threatened him first, then thought better of it. "I'll call you in a couple of days. Text me when you've landed."

"Forget it."

"Why do you always have to be like this, Jenny? You automatically assume I'm guilty and never give me a chance. It isn't fair and it isn't right. You're just like everyone else at the ranch today. Look at him, he's an ex-con. He must have done it. Who needs proof?"

She inhaled sharply. "You weren't entirely innocent, Quinn. You did get into a fight with that guy."

"A verbal altercation. Not physical."

She ignored him. "If you hadn't, he wouldn't have accused you, and you wouldn't have gone to prison."

"You think I don't know that? It haunts my dreams. But my mistake wasn't nearly as terrible as the ones committed against me, including those committed by the parents today and you if you keep Corrine from me." He paused, trying to slow his heart rate. "Give me a chance, Jenny. You owe me that much."

He thought for sure she'd say no and walk away, dragging Corrine behind her. Instead, some of what he'd said must have gotten through to her, for she nodded slowly. "One chance. One last chance."

Quinn was bothered by her attitude; however, he chose

not to antagonize her. Sometimes it was better to take a small victory and retreat until another day.

"Thank you. You won't regret it."

"We'd better go. The line is getting longer."

He didn't hug Jenny, but he did pick up Corrine and hold her close for several long moments.

"I'll see you soon, honey. I'll miss you."

"Goodbye," she said in his ear.

He consoled himself with the knowledge that October was only a couple months away and by then Corrine would learn he was her father.

He watched them until they were through the security checkpoint and out of sight. Then he left, hurrying through the airport and outside to the parking garage. He hardly noticed the people he passed or the cars stopping for him in the crosswalk.

At his truck, he pulled out his phone. He'd shut it off when he drove Jenny and Corrine to the airport, not wanting any interruptions. Once on, the phone displayed three missed calls, all of them from Summer. There were also two voice-mail messages.

He decided not to listen to them until he got home. His mind needed a rest before tackling the next set of problems, and the list was a lengthy one.

Regardless of how it turned out with the students' parents, Quinn could count on having lost his job with the therapy program. Even if the full story came to light, and he hoped it did, the parents wouldn't allow him within a mile of their kids. That left Quinn without any income and few opportunities.

He briefly recalled the conversation with Assistant Warden Tedrowe regarding the work release program. He'd yet to mention it to his cousins. Maybe he should.

Or not. Why was he even considering the job? If the

parents didn't want him, an innocent man, near their children, what would they think of a busload of prisoners? The idea was ludicrous.

At the next stoplight, Quinn scrolled through his call log for the assistant warden's number. Finding it, he placed a call just as traffic started to move and was eventually put through to an automated voice-mail system. He started out thanking the man for the opportunity, said he'd be leaving Mustang Valley and wouldn't be able to take the position, then ended by wishing the man luck in his search for another candidate and cattle ranch.

Leaving Mustang Valley? Until Quinn spoke the words out loud, he hadn't realized he'd made the decision to return home to his parents and grandparents. His grandfather had been after one of his grandchildren to come work for him and take over the family horse-breeding business. It was probably the best—and only—opportunity Quinn would have available.

At the next stoplight, he placed a call to his grandfather, who was delighted to hear from him and even more delighted to learn Quinn was thinking of coming home.

There was another person he needed to tell, and she deserved more than a phone brush off.

Summer answered on the second ring with a breathless, "Hi. How are you?"

"I've been better." Why lie?

"Jenny and Corrine get off okay?"

"They got off. I wouldn't say it went okay." He paused and cleared his throat. "If the offer's still open, I'd like to come over."

"Of course. When?"

"Seven?"

"You want dinner? We're having grilled cheese sandwiches. I'm afraid it's not much—"

"No dinner." In truth, he wasn't hungry. "Thanks, though."

"Should I take Teddy to the sitter's?"

"No." Quinn wanted to see the boy. It might be the last time.

"All right. Seven o'clock."

The hope in her voice was obvious even with a mediocre cell phone connection. Quinn hated hurting her, but the more he thought about it, the more he realized he had no choice.

SUMMER HADN'T ADMITTED to herself how nervous she was about Quinn coming over until the doorbell rang. She jerked in response, which was silly since he was right on time and she'd been watching the clock for the past hour.

Teddy beat her to the front door. She'd told him Quinn was coming but wasn't entirely sure he'd understood. Apparently, he had.

Opening the door, Teddy exclaimed, "Man," and hurled himself at Quinn.

"Hi, son. How you doing?" Quinn raised his arms, allowing Teddy to embrace his waist. "I missed you, too." Lowering a hand, he patted Teddy's head.

The affection in his voice touched Summer, and the lump already lodged in her throat doubled in size. Her son wasn't just fond of Quinn, he quite possibly loved him.

He might not be the only one. Summer was quite convinced she, too, had fallen for Quinn—which strengthened her determination to stand by him through thick and thin.

"Come in," she said, waiting for her hug. He didn't make a move toward her, not even when Teddy released him. After an awkward moment, she asked, "Can I get you something? A cold drink?"

"Water's fine."

They made their way to the kitchen. Summer had hurriedly cleaned the dishes after their grilled cheese dinner. She was about to offer Quinn a seat on the couch in the family room when he headed for the table and sat. Teddy stood behind him, his fingers hovering an inch above Quinn's shoulder.

Summer set a glass of ice water down in front of him before taking the adjacent chair. "Tell me what went wrong at the airport. You sounded down on the phone."

"Jenny gave me a hard time. First, she tried to refuse me future visitations with Corrine. Then she threatened to disappear again."

"No! She can't do that."

"Honestly, I doubt she will. Jenny's like that, prone to impulsiveness. Just look at her history."

"Except she's taken drastic measures. Once, at least," Summer pointed out. "You lost Corrine for three years."

"She has a good job in Seaside and a boyfriend she seems pretty attached to."

"He could go with her." She covered Quinn's hand with her own. "I don't mean to be negative, but I've seen the most unlikely parents disappear when under extreme stress."

"I made it clear to Jenny I'd take legal action if she did anything rash."

He went on to describe in detail his trip to the airport. Summer couldn't believe what she was hearing. From what Quinn said, Jenny hadn't changed one bit since she last saw him. Obviously, she was a good mother; one had only to look at Corrine to know that. But Jenny possessed a selfish streak a mile wide.

"Are you going to talk to Marty?" Summer asked.

"Tomorrow. First thing."

"I wouldn't dream of interfering, but I'd be glad to be a witness on your behalf."

"Let's see. Jenny said she was going to have her attorney investigate. I'd like to get a jump on him and start our own investigation."

"Good idea. I'll help any way I can."

He nodded. "Thanks."

She had the distinct impression there was more on his mind. Quinn confirmed her suspicions with his next words.

"Summer. We need to talk."

"Oh." She didn't like the ominous note in his voice and hated the panic in hers. "What's wrong?"

"I wanted to tell you right away. As soon as I made the decision. I owe you that much."

"You're leaving," she stated flatly.

"How did you know?"

"Déjà vu." His declaration sounded identical to the one Hal had made when he announced he'd filed for divorce.

"I have no choice," Quinn said. "The ranch depends on the money from the sanctuary and therapy program. Without it, they'll go broke."

"The parents won't pull their kids from the program. It's too valuable to them. Every single one has made progress."

"I think they will."

Summer paused and considered what to say next. She wanted—*needed*—Quinn to stay, yet she had no right to ask. One night together was hardly enough to base a future on and make a commitment.

Except, for Summer, it had been.

"I can't get a job anywhere in Mustang Valley," he said. "No one will hire me with a record."

"You have a job at Dos Estrellas."

"That pays only room and board. I need a regular salary if I hope to share custody of Corrine."

He was right. Nonetheless, Summer continued to try to sway him. "What about Marty? Will he represent you pro bono if you move?"

"I don't know. I'll ask him tomorrow."

"I'm sure Cole and Josh will want you to stay. They—"

"Summer, please. I know this is hard on you. It's hard on me, too. We've barely started, and to end things so quickly…"

The sincerity in his voice was her undoing. She couldn't answer him for fear of breaking down.

Teddy had abandoned Quinn's side and was now beneath the table at his feet. He sat cross-legged, rocking back and forth. He'd clearly understood enough of the conversation to realize Quinn's intentions.

Summer ached for her son and for Quinn. Mostly, she ached for herself.

If only she'd told Cara and Quinn about the petition when she had the chance. Did Quinn secretly blame her for everything? Of course he did. He should.

"Will you ever come back to Mustang Valley?" she asked softly.

"Eventually. I'm not sure when and how often."

She averted her gaze, worried he'd notice the hurt in her eyes. "What if you postponed leaving for a while?"

"We'd just be delaying the inevitable. I couldn't do that to you."

"I'm willing to take the chance."

"There's more than us to consider," he said.

"You mean Hal?" Summer pulled Quinn aside, out of Teddy's hearing range. "Don't worry, he's a lot of bark and little bite."

Quinn shook his head. "I disagree. I saw him today. Twice. He has a lot of bite."

"Whatever he says, he doesn't want Teddy. You saw,

he brought him home from the sitter's after less than an hour together."

"Doesn't mean he won't protect Teddy or cause trouble if I stick around. Deep down, he loves Teddy."

"He sure has a lousy way of showing it."

"Maybe he doesn't know how." Quinn spoke slowly. "You could help him."

Summer sat up. "You think I haven't tried?"

"Try again. Teddy's not a battleground. He deserves the love and support of both his parents."

My God! Could Quinn be right? Had Summer contributed to Teddy and Hal's strained relationship? Worse, was she the cause of it? The more she considered the possibility, the more she realized it was true.

Shame filled her, and regret. "I've behaved atrociously."

"You love Teddy. You've always tried to do what was best for him."

"It's not fair." She stared imploringly at Quinn. "Not to you, not to me and especially not to Teddy. Here I've finally found a guy who not only cares for me, he cares for my son. It's a minor miracle. Only I lose him after a few weeks because a group of people, Hal included, are narrow-minded and judgmental."

"Opinions that strong are nearly impossible to change, Summer. Trust me."

"They shouldn't be. I've fought this kind of prejudice the last four years, trying to get people to accept my son and his disability. I never thought I'd see a time when the same prejudice was directed at an innocent man."

"Your naivety is charming."

"And you're being sarcastic."

"A little."

She rubbed her temples, wondering if there was some

way she could intone a magic spell and reverse this day. Start all over, fresh. "Where are you going? Bishop?"

"Yeah. It's about a day's drive from Seaside. Close enough I can visit Corrine on weekends or Jenny can drive her down to see me and my family. My grandfather will give me a job wrangling horses until I either find something else or he convinces me to take over the business."

"That'll be nice for your parents. Having you home and being able to see Corrine." Summer just wished it wasn't so far from Mustang Valley.

He stood then, and, taking her hand, pulled her to her feet. Wrapping his arms around her, he held her close and rested his chin on her head. "My daughter and my cousins' well-being are the only reasons I'd leave you and Teddy. I swear it's true."

"I believe you." Summer struggled not to cry. "I won't stop you from going even though every part of me is screaming to do just that. Dammit," she muttered when the tears started to fall.

He pressed his lips to her hair. "Let's have none of that."

"When are you leaving?"

"Soon. The end of the week."

Five days. Surviving until Friday would be pure torture.

She clung to him, desperate because this was in all likelihood the last time. Even if she suggested they get together before Quinn left, he wouldn't agree.

"It's time." He put her gently aside.

She dabbed at her eyes with the back of her hand.

"I'd like to say goodbye to Teddy."

"Sure." Summer's chest constricted.

Quinn knelt down beside the table. "Hi, Teddy. You mind coming out from there?"

He stopped rocking and shook his head, his mouth set in a determined frown.

"I'd like to talk to you before I go."

"Staaa," Teddy blurted.

Summer covered her face with her hands, holding back the sobs. Her son hadn't taken to someone like he had Quinn since a young friend in his preschool class. Their emotional parting when Teddy had withdrawn in order to attend the learning center had also broken her heart.

"I can't, son." Quinn's voice cracked.

"Why?"

Summer gasped softly. Teddy was having a real conversation with Quinn. She also couldn't say that had happened since preschool.

So much improvement thanks to Quinn. Literally in the span of a month, he'd accomplished more with Teddy than all the therapists and teachers put together. How could fate be so kind to her in one way and so cruel in the other?

"It's hard to explain," Quinn said. "My daughter needs me. You remember Corrine? Well, I love her, like your mom loves you. I'm going to California so I can be closer to her and help raise her. Do you understand?"

He said nothing about the shameful treatment he'd received at the hands of the students' parents and Hal. That was so like Quinn.

Summer could literally feel her future hopes and dreams shattering, and the pain was indescribable. Reaching for the nearest handhold, in this case a chair back, she steadied herself.

All at once, Teddy crawled out from under the table. Quinn stood and drew the boy to his side, gathering him in a fierce hug.

"You take care of your mother, hear me?"

Teddy nodded.

"If I call, will you talk to me?"

Another nod.

"All right. Good, then." Quinn swallowed, and Summer thought there might be tears in his eyes.

She walked him to the door. She wanted to hurl herself at him like Teddy had done earlier. Somehow she managed to restrain herself.

"Do you really think we'll see each other again?" she asked.

"I'm counting on it."

"Promise me you'll call."

"Yes. But that's the only promise I'll make."

She should have been glad for his honesty. Silently, she begged him to lie to her. Tell her pretty stories about how they'd be together someday soon.

She sniffled. "Have a safe trip."

"I…"

"Yes?"

"Goodbye, Summer."

She watched him walk to his truck, parked beside the curb, his retreating form barely discernable in the dim glow of the solar yard lights.

Closing the door, she turned, her throat on fire, and came face-to-face with Teddy. He put his arms around her and laid his head on her tummy.

"Maw Maw."

Summer's knees nearly gave out. Thank goodness for the door.

Five years she'd been waiting for her son to willingly embrace her and express his love. Allow her to express her love in return.

It would have to be today.

Chapter Thirteen

Quinn rode out to the mustang sanctuary rather than drive. He wanted his last look of Dos Estrellas to be from the back of a horse, plodding easily along, rather than from the inside of a truck. He took his time, savoring every moment and every scene.

Mother Nature didn't disappoint. Vivid blue skies overhead, lush green mountains rising majestically in the distance, and the sweet smell of desert flora on the breeze were just a few of her offerings. He would remember this day always and carry it with him, locked inside his heart. These past weeks at the ranch had been the happiest he'd felt since before his arrest.

Behind him, the buckskin mare followed, her hooves stirring up dust on the dirt road with each step. She'd come a long way since Quinn had plucked her from the herd, showing potential to become a dependable ranch horse or pleasure mount for some lucky individual.

Too bad her training would temporarily cease. Quinn was returning her to the sanctuary until Cole had a break in his schedule and could pick up where Quinn left off, whenever that might be.

Both the borrowed gelding Quinn rode and the buckskin raised their heads and pricked their ears as the sanctuary came into sight. There weren't any mustangs to greet them, but the horses must have sensed the herd wasn't far off. Quinn figured on a few head showing up before he and the horses reached the gate.

The buckskin quickened her pace, her gaze riveted on the nearby rise. He'd yet to name her and thought maybe he should before he returned her to the sanctuary.

Lilac, he decided, choosing the same name Corrine had given her stuffed purple pony. Saying it out loud, he deemed the choice a good one.

Summer would have liked the name, too. He didn't have to concentrate hard to hear her laugh or see her smile. She was never very far from his thoughts as it was.

Damn, he missed her. Acutely. With a powerful longing that would have knocked him flat if he hadn't been riding.

There was no point dwelling on the past or punishing himself. Things happened for a reason, even if that reason wasn't immediately apparent. He was leaving Mustang Valley in order for the therapy program and sanctuary to continue, so that all of his cousins' hard work to restore Dos Estrellas these past ten months would not be wasted, and so he'd be closer to his daughter and be able to put the pieces of his life back together in some sort of meaningful order.

On a positive note, Jenny had called him yesterday and told him she was still planning on bringing Corrine to his parents' in October. She didn't apologize, not that he'd expected her to. But he swore he heard regret in her voice.

Neither had she mentioned the false accusations made against Quinn, though she must have heard the latest development. One of Marty's legal interns had questioned the mother of the boy who claimed Quinn manhandled him, along with several other parents. While the boy stuck to his story and his mother stood by him, he'd apparently bragged to the other children he'd been playing with that day about beating up Nathan.

Eventually, the full story had emerged, and Marty reported it to Jenny's attorney, including two statements from cooperative parents. The next day, Jenny had called Quinn.

It bothered him that she hadn't believed him from the start. Sadly, it would probably always be this way, him having to prove himself at each and every turn and not just with Jenny. Even in Bishop, the town where he grew up, there would be people ready to think the worst of him.

How different things had been with Summer. Other than his family, she'd been the one person to accept and defend him unquestioningly. Whether she did so because she was simply that kind of person or because she cared for him, he wasn't sure.

The ache inside him intensified. They'd seen each other only once these past four days. Quinn had been busy tying up loose ends and packing his few belongings for the drive to California. He saw no reason to add to their misery and, apparently, neither did Summer.

As she'd predicted, his cousins were turning the screws. They'd gone so far as to call their grandparents and ask them to talk some sense into Quinn. Their grandparents had listened but, in the end, chose not to get involved. Whether Quinn stayed or not was his decision. Thus far, he'd remained steadfast in his conviction that leaving was best for everyone involved.

As the gate to the sanctuary came into view, the horses' excitement increased. At the same moment, several mustangs appeared on the first rise, their long manes and tails blowing in the wind.

Quinn felt another emotional tug. They were quite the picture, a piece of living Arizona history.

"Your welcoming party has arrived," he said to the buckskin.

She whinnied, loudly and shrilly, and would have jumped the fence if not for his firm grip on the lead rope.

When they reached the gate, Quinn dismounted and undid the latch. He removed the halter from the mare and swung the gate wide. She bolted through it and galloped up the rise to join the other mustangs, the gelding staring after them.

Quinn gave him a friendly pat. "Maybe one of these days you and I will both come back."

A surge raced through Quinn as realization dawned. Like the mare, he, too, was free. Not so many months ago, he'd sat in a tiny cell, not daring to consider life outside prison for six or more years. And while he was leaving a wonderful woman he'd come to care for more than he'd imagined possible, he did have a daughter and a job and his freedom. It was something denied a lot of men in his shoes.

His return trip to the ranch went a little faster, with the gelding picking up speed as the outbuilding came into sight. None too soon, either, for the sun had just started to set. Within minutes, the desert went from tarnished gold to bathed in the soft inky light of dusk. A last gift from Mother Nature.

Quinn neared the outskirts of the horse pastures. Cutting across those, he came upon the gate leading to the pens. The tractor was parked there, having been left by one of the hands this morning after grading the arena.

All at once, the gelding spooked. Twisting in a sharp half circle, he darted to the left. Quinn hung on, putting his weight in his heels and squeezing with his legs.

"Whoa, boy!"

The horse stopped and stood but remained tense, his hide twitching. Quinn looked around for what had alarmed the normally tranquil horse. Seeing nothing, he prodded the horse forward. They got only a few feet when Quinn heard what sounded like crying and drew up on the reins.

The sound *was* crying, and it came from the other side of the tractor.

He got off the horse, dropped the reins and approached. "Who's there? Are you all right?"

The crying promptly diminished to a whimper. Quinn caught a movement from behind the left rear tire.

He hurried around the tractor, and when he caught sight of a small boy crouched into a ball, he came to a halt.

"Hey, buddy."

The boy crouched lower, if that was possible, and peeked at Quinn through splayed fingers.

"I won't hurt you." He advanced slowly, recognizing the boy as one of the therapy program students. "Got lost, huh?"

The boy nodded.

"You remember me?"

He shrugged.

"I work here. My name's Quinn. What's yours?"

"Brett." He made a noise between a hiccup and a sharp laugh. Quinn also noticed the boy's rapidly blinking eyes.

"Come on out. Let me take you back. I'm sure your parents are looking for you."

Brett shook his head, his blinking increasing.

Quinn suddenly remembered. He was the son of the woman—Mindy?—who'd rallied the parents against him. Brett had… What was it called? Tourette's syndrome.

"I promise, Brett, you have nothing to be afraid of. I won't hurt you."

He looked less afraid but didn't move.

"You like horses?"

He hiccupped again.

"Tell you what. You come out, and I'll let you lead this one back to the stables. What do you say?"

His eyes widened. Quinn didn't dare rush him, afraid he might run away.

"Your mom must be worried."

After several more minutes of coaxing and reassurances, Quinn was able to lure Brett out from behind the tractor. They started walking, the boy leading the horse. Quinn thought he saw zigzagging flashlights ahead. Keeping up a constant and, he hoped, reassuring banter, he removed his phone and dialed Cara.

"I found Brett in the arena by the tractor," he said when she answered.

"Oh, thank God. We've been looking for him for twenty minutes. Mindy's frantic."

"We're almost there."

Cara disconnected without saying goodbye. Seconds later, Quinn heard shouting and then saw the outline of people running toward them—Cara, Mindy and two of the therapy program staff members.

Mindy reached them first. She grabbed up Brett and hugged him to her, sobbing incoherently.

"Thank you, Quinn." Cara threw an arm around him.

"Just glad he's okay." Taking the lead rope, he waved at the boy and started off, the horse following.

"Wait," Mindy called.

Quinn stopped. Turned.

"I heard…the other children admitted you didn't hurt that boy. I'm…sorry I misjudged you."

He could see on her face the admission and apology weren't easy. Which made him appreciate the gesture all the more.

"No worries." He tugged on the brim of his cowboy hat and continued to the horse stables.

He was just brushing down the gelding when Josh and Cole showed up. Quinn didn't think much of it. This was probably a last-ditch effort at getting him to reconsider.

"Heard you're the hero of the day," Josh said.

"No big deal. I happened to be riding by the tractor and heard the kid crying."

"You do know who his mom is, right?"

"Yeah." Quinn returned the brush to the hook on the wall outside the tack room.

"She's going around telling everyone she made a mistake and that you didn't mistreat any children."

"Okay."

Cole clapped him on the shoulder. "Come on, man. This is what we've been waiting for. You can keep your job."

Quinn untied the gelding and started down the barn aisle, Josh and Cole dogging his heels.

"It's not that simple." He put the horse in his stall and shut the door.

"But she admitted the truth," Josh said. "Everyone will know by tomorrow."

"Nothing's changed." Quinn faced his cousins. "I still have a reputation that will follow me regardless. I'm better off at Granddad and Grandma's. There, at least, I have family."

"What are we?" Cole asked. "Strangers? Hell, we grew up together."

"I appreciate all you've done for me. Honestly."

"Why didn't you tell us about Assistant Warden Tedrowe and the work release program?" Josh asked, mild accusation in his voice.

That took Quinn aback. "How do you know?"

"He called. Right after you rode out of here for the sanctuary."

"I'm sorry. I should have mentioned it." They stood in

front of the stall, the bright fluorescent overhead lights humming noisily and attracting dozens of nighttime insects. "But I'd already decided to leave and Tedrowe said the only way the program would work was with a former inmate in charge."

"It wasn't just your decision to make. We should have been consulted."

"You're right." Quinn hung his head. "I'm sorry. It was a tough week, and I had a lot on my mind."

"Like Summer?"

"Leaving her isn't easy."

"Look," Josh said, "we're moving the therapy program to the Small Change."

"Reese's father's place?" Quinn stared at them in disbelief. "Why?"

"Cara, Cole and I have talked this over, and we're in complete agreement."

"All this in the last hour?"

Cole grinned. "Good decisions don't take long to make."

"It's a worthwhile program," Josh went on. "For the ranch and for the prisoners. The assistant warden explained they wouldn't be sending hardcore criminals. Just guys deserving of a second chance. You can relate to that."

Quinn thought his cousin was laying on the guilt a little thick.

"When we called Theo about moving the therapy program, he was immediately on board. He's willing to donate some of the Small Change's facilities in exchange for a tax write-off. That way, Cara gets to keep the therapy program, and the students won't be within miles of the prisoners. Everyone benefits."

"Can Dos Estrellas handle the loss of income?" Quinn asked.

"We'll more than make up for it with the free labor from

the work release program. Besides, the mustang sanctuary will remain here, and Cara will still cover her portion of the property taxes and expenses."

"You've got to take the job." Cole gave Quinn's shoulder another clap. "The state will pay you far more than the therapy program did. Think how that will help your custody suit."

"I told Granddad I'd work for him."

"He has plenty of help," Josh said. "And if you want, you can take six weeks off over the summer to stay with him out in California while you have Corrine. She'll love all the horses."

Quinn liked the idea and hoped Jenny would, too.

"You're going to make a real difference in people's lives. Become the kind of person your daughter will be proud to call Dad."

Going to? Josh was talking like Quinn had already accepted the job.

"I don't know. I'm leaving tomorrow."

"You still have tonight to think about it. Assistant Warden Tedrowe said you could call him if you have any questions. He gave us his private cell phone number." Josh glanced past Quinn's shoulder and smiled as if he knew something Quinn didn't.

A moment later, he realized his cousin did indeed know something. Summer stood at the end of the barn aisle, a nervous look on her face. Quinn thought his heart might explode.

"What are you waiting for, man?" Josh gave him a nudge. "Go talk to the lady."

EVERYTHING WAS DECIDED, Quinn thought. He had a plan in motion that would spare the people he cared about difficulties and enable him to pursue a relationship with Corrine by living and working at a place that met Jenny's approval.

Yet, here he was walking toward Summer and knowing, deep inside, he was about to break all the promises he'd made to himself. How could he not when she stared at him with feelings he recognized and was afraid would fade too quickly?

"Quinn," she said as he neared, and he heard the same emotion in her voice that he saw in her eyes. "I heard about what happened. You found Brett."

News apparently traveled very fast.

"Cara called me," she said.

"It's no big deal."

"It's a very big deal." Summer reached for him. At the last second, she let her hands drop. "There isn't a single parent in the program who hasn't realized what a terrible mistake they made. I'd expect a formal apology if I were you."

"I didn't help Brett for an apology."

"Of course not. But the parents need to issue it, and you should let them."

"The kid wasn't far," Quinn said. "He'd have found his way back eventually. Probably in a matter of minutes."

"Maybe. Or he might have wandered off and gotten even more lost. Let the parents apologize. You deserve it."

"I was planning on being long gone by morning."

"Don't leave." Summer took a step toward him. It wasn't much. A few inches. But, then, sometimes a few inches was the greatest distance in the world. "Not yet, anyway. Give me and Teddy a chance to convince you to stay."

"I already told Jenny I was moving."

"I would never ask you to choose me and Teddy over Corrine. I'm only hoping there's room in your heart for all of us."

"How much room there is in my heart isn't the problem."

"We're worth fighting for."

Hadn't he said the same thing to himself not long ago?

"Cara told me about the job offer and the work release program. She said they're relocating the therapy program to the Small Change."

"Jenny wouldn't like me working with prisoners. I couldn't stand it if she took Corrine away from me again."

"She'd have to prove you're a threat to Corrine. She can't, and no judge will side with her."

Quinn heard Summer's words, but they didn't alleviate his anxiety. "I want to stay, I really do. I just can't stop worrying."

"Is there no compromise you can reach?"

"Possibly. Josh suggested we suspend the work release program from June through August and that I spend that time in Bishop at our grandparents' with Corrine."

"That's not a bad idea."

"No, it's not." He glanced away.

"What do *you* want, Quinn?" She touched his arm. "If you could take Jenny and the therapy program parents and your fight to clear your record and everything else negative out of the equation, where would you go and what would you do?"

He thought a moment.

"I'd take the job with the prison release program. I'd be good at it and could make a difference in people's lives." He turned back to her. "I'd date you. I'd set out to convince you I'm the guy you've been waiting for."

She smiled, and her eyes shone with the same emotion from earlier. "You wouldn't have to work hard. I'm already convinced."

"I'd take you and Teddy to Bishop with me over summer vacation so that the four of us could be a family."

"I'm sure I could work it out with Marty."

"And when I'd won my settlement from the state, I'd put enough money away for Corrine's college education, pay Jenny child support and take you on a Caribbean cruise."

Tears filled her eyes.

"Except I'm not sure about any of that. Circumstances are against us."

Summer lifted her arms and circled Quinn's neck. "You're wrong. They're working in our favor. Fate is trying to tell us she approves."

Quinn held her closer, feeling the world right itself. This was where he belonged, where he'd belonged all along.

"That's quite the romantic notion."

She smiled, lighting up not only her face but the last dark corner in his heart. "What can I say? I happen to be a hopeless romantic."

"There's still Hal," Quinn said. "He doesn't want me near Teddy."

"Hal has, shall we say, had an epiphany, probably due to his wife."

"Tell me."

"He and I have started seeing a counselor. A mediator, actually. Hal's attorney made the recommendation. I'm supporting Hal's more frequent and lengthier visits with Teddy by coaching Teddy and guiding Hal. He, his wife and I will attend parenting sessions together at the learning center."

"That's good. And not just for us." Quinn tugged her closer.

"I haven't always been fair to Hal," she admitted.

"He was a fool to let you and Teddy go."

Summer tilted her face to Quinn's. "His loss could be your gain."

"Are you sure Hal won't take action?"

She shook her head. "He doesn't have a leg to stand on. His attorney advised him to back down."

"That's no guarantee."

"He won't fight you, Quinn. You have to trust me on this."

"I do trust you. Mostly."

"What can I do to convince you?"

He bent his head and rested his cheek against hers. "There's one last thing I need."

"What?" she murmured.

"I want to hear you say it, Summer. There's been too much uncertainty, too many things gone wrong in my life these last three years, for me to make assumptions when it comes to how much you care for me."

"Okay." She nodded. "Here goes. I'm falling in love with you, and I think you're falling in love with me, too."

"You're right." He grinned. "Very astute."

"Comes from having an autistic son. I need to be aware of even the smallest details."

"You rescued me, Summer. Brought me back from a place no one should be and showed me how to be happy."

"Aren't you ever going to kiss me?" She parted her lips.

He savored the slight intake of her breath when he claimed her mouth and enjoyed her sigh of contentment even more. He considered holding her indefinitely, but that wasn't an option, and he reluctantly released her.

No matter, they'd have time tonight.

"We're going to be happy together." Summer laid her head on his chest.

Quinn didn't fool himself. The road ahead was bumpy

and laden with potholes. He was okay with that, as long as he traveled the road with Summer.

"Are you going to call the assistant warden and accept the job offer?" she asked.

"Tomorrow."

"First thing?"

"Later. I have other plans, including breakfast with my girlfriend."

"Girlfriend?"

He pressed a last kiss to her lips. "I've missed you."

"I've missed you, too. What do you say we not do this again?"

Linking fingers, they rounded the corner of the horse stables. Teddy was there, waiting with Cara. The moment he spotted Summer and Quinn, he broke into an awkward run.

"Kin, Kin."

It took him a moment to realize Teddy had called him by name. "Hey, son."

Teddy grabbed both Quinn and Summer's wrist and met their gazes for a little longer than usual. The three of them stood there for some time before finally letting go.

Only Corrine was missing from this otherwise perfect day. Soon enough, though, he'd see her, and she'd learn he was her father.

Then his life would be complete and his future bright, none of which would have been possible without the incredible woman standing beside him.

Epilogue

Fourteen months later

Raquel sat on the bench in the front courtyard, the one by the cactus garden where they'd spread her beloved August's ashes on this day two years ago. It was where she felt closest to him and not because this was his final resting place. This bench was where they'd talked, argued, laughed and professed their love.

"You would be proud of your sons," she said in a soft voice.

She frequently spoke to August, certain he could hear her, and more than once she'd been caught. Nathan and Kimberly's confusion when she tried to explain herself was cute to watch. Gabe always got a sad look on his face.

"No baby yet for Gabe and Reese. I suppose I shouldn't worry, they haven't been married long. And Reese wants to work a couple more years at the bank before starting a family. They'll do what they will in their own time—all my fretting won't make a difference."

Raquel sighed expansively and pulled her jacket collar tighter against a sudden breeze sweeping across the courtyard.

"They weren't happy at first when you left the three of them the ranch, let me tell you." She shook her head and tsked. "But Gabe, Cole and Josh are real brothers now. They love and support each other as if they grew up together instead of two states apart. Gabe is living at the Small Change and running the ranch full-time. Poor Theo's Parkinson's is advancing and he's almost entirely housebound. But I suppose you know that."

She felt her only son's absence acutely, even though he was a ten-minute drive away. For years, it had been just her, Gabe and August. The three of them against the world.

"He's happy, though," Raquel continued, smiling to herself, "and that is what counts. Josh runs Dos Estrellas and does a good job." She chuckled. "Okay, you're right. A great job. You wouldn't believe the only cattle he'd seen before coming here were calves and steers at the rodeo. He and Cara have a baby boy. Oh, he looks just like Josh. Nathan and Kimberly adore him and tell everyone they meet they're his big brother and big sister."

The sun slipped in and out of the wispy clouds, alternately casting Raquel in light and shadow.

"The mustang sanctuary and therapy program are bigger than ever." She gasped softly. "Did you see Cara on television last week? She won an award for her efforts to protect and promote wild horses in the southwest. I think that's how they said it." She placed a hand over heart. "She was beautiful and so humble when she accepted the award. I cried like a baby.

"And speaking of babies." Raquel sat up straighter. "Did you ever see a more beautiful one than Cole and Violet's? That little girl is an angel sent straight from heaven. I don't know when I've ever seen such a happy family. Well, except for us, my love. Violet decided to keep working part-time—she adores watching the baby. That makes Cole the official livestock manager. He seems to like horse training and putting on those roping clinics."

A low rumble in the distance drew Raquel's attention, and she looked toward the east. The bus from the prison in Florence had arrived, making its way down the road to pick up the work crew and return them to Florence.

"Prisoners on Dos Estrellas." Raquel lifted one shoulder. "Who would have guessed?"

She'd had her doubts in the beginning, even though Gabe staunchly supported the work release program. Well, she'd been wrong more than once in her life. The program was a booming success for both the ranch and the workers. One former prisoner who had been guilty of fraud was released last month after working six months for the Dempseys. He'd landed a job at a ranch in New Mexico as a result of the program. Raquel supposed everyone deserved a second chance.

"That Quinn," she continued. "You never met him, which is a shame. He might have been born here, the way he's taken to this ranch and the cattle business. He and Summer just announced their engagement. About time is all I have to say. Teddy's a regular fixture here." Raquel's heart melted. "He calls me Bella. That's the closest he can come to saying *Abuella*."

She spent some part of most days watching one child or another. Often several at once. Nothing made her happier.

"Did I tell you I decided to move into the guest suite? This house is too big and too empty for just me. Josh, Cara and the three children are moving in. They keep insisting they don't want to kick me out, as Cara says, and I keep insisting I want them to have the house. Really, I think I'll be fine in the guest suite. And, besides, it's time for the next generation of Dempseys to take over Dos Estrellas."

The sun emerged from behind another cloud, bathing Raquel in vivid sunlight. In the distance, cattle lowed, a horse whinnied and starlings chirped.

All was right and as it should be, she decided. What August hadn't accomplished in life, he'd accomplished in the two years since his passing. The ranch was thriving and would pass on to a fifth generation, old wounds were healed, and the Dempsey brothers and Quinn had become a close-knit and loving family, bound by not just blood, but adversity.

Raquel was confident they would endure always, an integral part of this valley community and the people in it.

* * * * *

MILLS & BOON®

Cherish™

EXPERIENCE THE ULTIMATE RUSH OF FALLING IN LOVE

MILLS & BOON®

EXCLUSIVE EXCERPT

When Dea Caracciolo agrees to attend a sporting event as tycoon Guido Rossano's date, sparks fly!

Read on for a sneak preview of
THE BILLIONAIRE'S PRIZE
the final instalment of Rebecca Winters'
thrilling Cherish trilogy
THE MONTINARI MARRIAGES

The dark blue short-sleeved dress with small red poppies Dea was wearing hugged her figure, then flared from the waist to the knee. With every step the material danced around her beautiful legs, imitating the flounce of her hair she wore down the way he liked it. Talk about his heart failing him!

"Dea—"

Her searching gaze fused with his. "I hope it's all right." The slight tremor in her voice betrayed her fear that she wasn't welcome. If she only knew...

"You've had an open invitation since we met." Nodding his thanks to Mario, he put his arm around her shoulders and drew her inside the suite.

He slid his hands in her hair. "You're the most beautiful sight this man has ever seen." With uncontrolled hunger he lowered his mouth to hers and began to devour her. Over the announcer's voice and the roar of the crowd, he heard her little moans of pleasure as their bodies merged and they drank deeply.

When she swayed in his arms, he half carried her over to the couch where they could give in to their frenzied needs. She smelled heavenly. One kiss grew into another until she became his entire world. He'd never known a feeling like this and lost track of time and place.

"Do you know what you do to me?" he whispered against her lips with feverish intensity.

"I came for the same reason."

Her admission pulled him all the way under. Once in a while the roar of the crowd filled the room, but that didn't stop him from twining his legs with hers. He desired a closeness they couldn't achieve as long as their clothes separated them.

"I want you, *bellissima*. I want you all night long. Do you understand what I'm saying?"

Don't miss
THE BILLIONAIRE'S PRIZE
by Rebecca Winters

Available November 2016

www.millsandboon.co.uk

ive a 12 month subscription to a friend today!

Call Customer Services
0844 844 1358*

or visit
illsandboon.co.uk/subscriptions

MILLS & BOON®

Why shop at millsandboon.co.uk?

Each year, thousands of romance readers find their perfect read at millsandboon.co.uk. That's because we're passionate about bringing you the very best romantic fiction. Here are some of the advantages of shopping at www.millsandboon.co.uk:

* **Get new books first**—you'll be able to buy your favourite books one month before they hit the shops

* **Get exclusive discounts**—you'll also be able to buy our specially created monthly collections, with up to 50% off the RRP

* **Find your favourite authors**—latest news, interviews and new releases for all your favourite authors and series on our website, plus ideas for what to try next

* **Join in**—once you've bought your favourite books, don't forget to register with us to rate, review and join in the discussions

Visit **www.millsandboon.co.uk**
for all this and more today!

MILLS_WEB